"All right, so I got lost. Who could blame me!"

Eden decided protective defiance was the best approach to Court's unexpected rescue. "The whole damned area is a mass of tire marks leading in all directions!"

"So, why didn't you use the map?" was Court's caustic greeting. "Or do you think that just because the men seem to have taken a shine to you, they'd be only too willing to spend their time searching for you?"

"No! That isn't it at all!" Eden protested vehemently, hurt that he could think this. "And if the men have 'taken a shine' to me," she added self-consciously, "it's not because I deliberately set out to win them over."

"Mmm, that's what makes it so bloody disturbing!" Court growled. "However, it wasn't my intention to sit here discussing your numerous conquests of the opposite sex. I suggest we concentrate on finding our way back to the homestead."

Kerry Allyne developed wanderlust after emigrating with her family from England to Australia. A long working holiday enabled her to travel the world before returning to Australia where she met her engineer husband-to-be. After marriage and the birth of two children, the family headed north to Summerland, a popular surfing resort, where they run a small cattle farm and an electrical contracting business. Kerry Allyne's travel experience adds much to the novels she spends her days writing—when, that is, she's not doing company accounts or herding cattle!

Books by Kerry Allyne

HARLEQUIN ROMANCE

Don't miss any of our special offers. Write to us at the following address for information on our newest releases.

Harlequin Reader Service
901 Fuhrmann Blvd., P.O. Box 1397, Buffalo, NY 14240
Canadian address: P.O. Box 603,
Fort Erie, Ont. L2A 5X3

Carpentaria Moon

Kerry Allyne

Harlequin Books

**TORONTO • NEW YORK • LONDON
AMSTERDAM • PARIS • SYDNEY • HAMBURG
STOCKHOLM • ATHENS • TOKYO • MILAN**

Original hardcover edition published in 1987
by Mills & Boon Limited

ISBN 0-373-02869-5

Harlequin Romance first edition November 1987

CHAPTER ONE

'So what do you think of it?' enquired Alick Seaton conversationally of the girl of some twenty-two years seated behind the wheel of the small sedan they were travelling in as they finally approached their destination on the lower, eastern shores of the Gulf of Carpentaria in Australia's far north.

'Well, I know you told me Arrunga River Station was on the Gulf, but I must admit I still didn't expect the outlook to be quite this beautiful,' Eden Challinor enthused, her sense of pleasurable anticipation growing at the thought of taking up her new position as Tourist Manager on the property.

Arrunga River had long been among the leaders of those operational cattle stations that had opened their gates to tourists wanting to experience life in the outback first-hand, but even so, she still hadn't been quite prepared for the sight that met her eyes on leaving behind the almost park-like scenery of tall golden grass dotted with bloodwoods, melaleucas, and pandanus trees they had been passing, and emerging on to a low grassy plateau.

To their left the grass sloped gently downwards to the white sands of the beach that edged the shallow, aquamarine waters of the Gulf, while ahead of them the white-painted homestead—high-set for coolness, as most were in the tropics—and numerous associated buildings lay within brightly coloured and carefully tended gardens. There was even a swimming pool, Eden noted, as well as a huge and well-utilised camping area beyond the gardens. Behind the buildings were also a number of cattle and horse yards, and to the north a long, wide airstrip.

Dragging her gaze away from the sparkling sea as they neared the first of the many outbuildings, she went on in a slightly more doubtful tone, 'Nor was I expecting there to be such a large number of people here either, to be honest.' There was a surprising number of tents and vehicles, including a touring coach, in the camping area alone, and although she might have had some years of practice in dealing with the public as a receptionist she had the feeling that where this many people were concerned it could be a task of another order. 'I do wish you could have been just a little more specific as to what my duties are going to be.'

In actual fact, she had been taken by surprise altogether when, out of the blue, Alick—a casual acquaintance of some years' standing due to the firm of solicitors for whom Eden had previously worked having occupied offices above his stock and station agency in Townsville—had first approached her with the idea of taking on the position of Tourist Manager on his younger stepbrother's property.

However, as a result of what she had heard and read about Arrunga River Station, plus her own fascination to know more about life in such remote areas, she had accepted his offer without hesitation despite his only vague references as to her duties. His suggestion that she might also like to try her hand at preparing an advertising brochure for the property, brought about by his knowledge that her long-standing hobby was photography, was merely an extra incentive as far as she was concerned.

Now, before answering, Alick looked away, raising a hand in greeting to a man coming out of what appeared to be a machine shed. 'Sorry, sweetie, I thought it best to let Court decide that,' he advised in casual tones, referring to his stepbrother.

Eden's winged brows peaked eloquently. 'He doesn't already know?'

'No—well. . .' He paused, a rueful grin lighting his pleasant-featured face. 'To tell the truth, he doesn't even know he has a Tourist Manager yet. *I* was the one who decided he needed one.'

'You mean. . .!'

'Just pull up under that tree over there,' he interrupted to direct, as if she hadn't broken into gasping speech. 'Then we'll go and find out where everyone is.'

Eden did as suggested mechanically, if rather less than smoothly, and scrambled from the car herself when he promptly alighted. 'Alick!' she immediately began to protest. 'You said he'd asked you to arrange for. . .'

'No, that was just with regard to a photographer,' he broke in on her with an unperturbed smile and a shrug. 'The rest was all my own idea. . .because he's too damned independent, or stubborn, to admit he could do with a lessening of his involvement in that area.'

'All of which now makes my present position that much more doubtful!' she lamented in part annoyance, part dismay, her previous experience in the commercial photographic field being exactly zero. 'How can I possibly stay here knowing. . .'

'Hey, don't let it worry you,' Alick interposed yet again, dropping an arm about her shoulders and giving her an encouraging squeeze. 'It'll be okay, you'll see. After all, he'll be getting two for the price of one, as it were. So just trust your Uncle Alick, huh?'

Eden cast him a highly ironical glance. 'If you don't mind my saying so, it's beginning to appear as if I've trusted *Uncle* Alick too much already!'

He shook his head in feigned reproval. 'That's gratitude for you, I must say,' he grinned, starting to propel her along with him towards the doorway leading into the long, low building nearest them. 'And you're obviously underrating my powers of persuasion. In any case, Court won't turn you off the place, so to speak. He never has anyone before. He's a good bloke, and you'll like him, I'm sure.'

More to the point, perhaps, would *he* like having her apparently thrust into his employ uninvited—and unwanted? wondered Eden dubiously as they entered the building. That was, if he didn't adamantly veto the idea altogether, of course!

Inside, they passed a couple of closed doors, one designated *Office* and the other *Kitchen*, before entering a spacious area that opened on to the gardens and swimming pool, and which was set with padded stools around a wood-inlaid bar as well as a number of tables and chairs, together with a snooker table. Through an archway decorated with stock-whips and branding irons and the bleached skull of what must have been a massive crocodile, Eden only had time to make out a flower-adorned dining-room before her attention was returned to the bar as Alick headed them towards the seats that lined it.

The tall, willowy black-haired girl in her middle twenties who had just finished serving three men a little further along—the only other patrons at that early time of the afternoon—now turned in the new-comers' direction, her brows lifting expressively as her dark gaze came to rest on Alick.

'Well, well, look who just blew in,' she mocked with obvious familiarity on coming to a halt in front of them. 'You taken to escorting your—um—old friends all the way out here now, Alick?'

'Hello to you too, Crystal.' His response was drily made. 'And no, I haven't taken to escorting my friends, old or otherwise, out here. For your information, I've offered Eden a job at Arrunga River. . . as Tourist Manager.'

A statement that had a sardonic half-laugh promptly ensuing. 'Well, that's certainly a novel approach—even for you. Unfortunately, though, I don't believe we have a vacancy for any such position,' the tall girl smiled with noticeable smugness.

'Naturally not. . . now it's been filled,' Alick returned smoothly. 'And that being the case, I guess an introduction to your new superior would be appropriate. Crystal Lamont—Eden Challinor.' He performed the introductions with a certain relish.

Eden also suspected his choice of words had been deliberate—he had certainly never mentioned anything to her about the likelihood of her being in charge of any of the other staff—but despite not having been able to quite grasp the meaning of some of their exchanges, or the cause for the evident under-current between them, she was anxious to put her best foot forward and so smiled in a friendly fashion as she prepared to acknowledge the other girl.

Before she could do so, however, Crystal, who apparently felt no such inclination to be sociable, ignored her overture completely in favour of break-ing into repudiating speech.

'Court's my only boss!' she stated in frigid, super-
cilious accents. 'Not to mention also being the *only*
one with the authority to hire staff for this property!
And since *he* has never displayed the slightest interest in employing anyone in such a capacity. . .' She
shrugged significantly and allowed herself another
self-satisfied smile. 'Moreover, the staff quarters are
already full to overflowing at the moment, with no
likelihood of any vacancies in the foreseeable future
either.'

'Then I suppose Eden will simply have to move
into the homestead,' Alick proposed ironically, evidently not about to permit the other girl to deter him.
'There's certainly plenty of spare rooms there, and it
would seem to be fitting to her position.'

'The homestead!' Crystal exclaimed half incredulously, half furiously. 'But even *I'm* not quartered
there!'

'Although not for the want of trying,' he wasn't
averse to mocking.

A dark flush mounted Crystal's cheeks and a dire-
ful glitter entered her brown eyes, but when she would
have stormed back to the other end of the bar, Alick
forestalled her with a wryly voiced, 'Oh, before you
go, we'll have a drink, thanks.' He turned to Eden.
'What would you like?'

'Oh—er—just an orange juice, please,' she relayed
vaguely, her thoughts still occupied with, and disturbed by the sometimes enigmatic, but definitely less
than amiable conversation she had just heard.

'And I'll have my usual,' Alick advised the girl
behind the bar, who provided the required refresh-
ments cursorily before departing to attend to the
other patrons of the bar once more.

Taking a thirst-quenching mouthful of her drink, Eden sighed dejectedly. 'More than ever I'm beginning to get the impression I should have stayed in Townsville,' she murmured. 'At least I did have a job there.'

'And I told you not to worry about it,' Alick reminded her with a cheering smile. He sent a brief glance down the bar. 'In any event, I wouldn't pay too much attention to what Crystal has to say, if I were you. Just because she's been here longer than the majority of the staff she may like to act as if her word's law, she may even believe it is, but she still doesn't have quite as much say as to what takes place as she imagines, believe me. There's only one person in charge here. . .'

'I know. . . your stepbrother, Court.' Eden pulled a rueful moue. 'And you said yourself, he doesn't *want* a Tourist Manager.'

'Then it will just be up to the two of us to convince him otherwise, won't it?'

'The two of us! What on earth could I possibly say that might be likely to change his mind? It's not even as if I've had any experience in similar work elsewhere. In fact, apart from your sketchy description, "to relieve your stepbrother of the responsibility of ensuring that the property's visitors have an enjoyable and smoothly run stay", I'm not even certain just what the position's supposed to entail!'

'At the moment, what does it matter?' he countered so blithely that she almost choked on her drink. 'Just stand your ground and refuse to be daunted, that's all.'

All! Was he serious? 'I wasn't aware an unrequested applicant had any ground, as such, to stand on!' Eden retorted with hollow glibness. 'Although I am starting to understand why you insisted on accompanying me when I came out here.'

For the first time, Alick looked apologetic. 'Yes, well, I'm sorry for keeping you in the dark for so long, even though it is on Court's behalf.'

'Then why didn't you work it out with him over the phone, or something, before offering me the position?'

His expression assumed a wry cast. 'Have you ever tried to conduct a discussion of that kind over the radio not only with anyone who cares to listening in, but never being able to cut in at crucial points either because the other person's still transmitting?' He expelled a long breath, shaking his head. 'Let me tell you, it's as good as impossible!'

'So you decided to present him—well, hopefully at least—with a *fait accompli* instead,' she deduced with a grimace. 'But why me? And. . .' a chance remembrance abruptly occurred to her, 'just what did Crystal mean, anyway, about it being a novel approach, even for you?'

'Oh, that was nothing,' he dismissed airily. 'She was simply having a shot at me over past matters. As you no doubt realised, we don't precisely hit it off together real well.'

Eden nodded, and then, because she had always found him very pleasant and easygoing, hazarded curiously, 'For any particular reason?'

'Mmm, mainly because she's a haughty bitch who isn't averse to using *any* method in order to get her own way on occasion! So take heed. . . she's one person whose bite can be worse than their bark.'

'Oh, beaut!' Eden applauded sarcastically. 'How can I ever repay you for getting me involved in all this?' She shook her head despairingly and raised her eyes skywards. 'Why me, oh lord? Why me?'

Alick laughed. 'Because I knew you reasonably well; I considered you had the right qualities to make a go of it; and for a bonus, you also happen to be one of the prettiest girls I've never dated.'

'And we all know just how few there are of those left in Townsville these days, don't we?' she quipped mockingly. The number of women Alick Seaton had managed to romance over the years had often been a source of disbelief, and wry amusement, to the girls in the offices upstairs. With his obviously roving eye, it was just as well he had never married, they had concluded. 'Nor, might I add, could I ever really be considered pretty,' she went on to dispute in dry, deprecating accents. She certainly had never thought so. 'My colouring's always been—well, not to put too fine a point on it—too unconventional, for that.'

Momentarily, Alick didn't comment as he scanned the gamine-styled, bronze-coloured hair with its feathery half-fringe that framed the contours of her heart-shaped face, noting the considerably darker brows and curling lashes that outlined the widely spaced tawny-gold eyes, the slender tiptilted nose above the generous, curving mouth, the clear, honey-tones skin that created such a warm and sensuous effect.

'You're right. . . you're not pretty,' he agreed at length. 'You're bloody beautiful, if you must now.' He grinned. 'And that's from an expert on the subject!'

Eden half smiled self-consciously. She hadn't been fishing for compliments—she *had* always considered her colouring too unusual for prettiness—nor had she expected him to pay her any.

'Yes, well,' she began in carefully controlled tones as she deposited her now empty glass on the counter and prepared to change the subject. 'Perhaps we should go and see your stepbrother now and try to settle the matter of whether I do have a job here or not. It would seem the most appropriate course to take, don't you think?'

'Except that I doubt he'll be around the homestead at this time of day,' Alick shrugged, and drained the last of his beer. 'Nevertheless, we can go and make sure. I suspect it would be a waste of time asking *her* his whereabouts.' An explicit nod was directed towards the end of the bar as he rose to his feet. 'At the moment she'd probably pretend not to know, or else send us on a wild goose chase. We'll doubtless find someone who can tell us, though.' He began leading the way out of the bar. 'And if Court isn't around we can spend the time unpacking and having a look over the place.'

Eden merely nodded. As much as she was interested in doing the latter, she wasn't at all sure she should go to the trouble of unpacking until she knew for certain that she would be staying, but she refrained from saying as much, surmising that she would only receive another recommendation to stop worrying.

In lieu, she averred, 'I certainly wouldn't mind getting my camera gear out of the heat. Even though the car's in the shade, it's still a little too hot to leave the film, especially, there any longer than is absolutely necessary.'

'In that case, we may as well deposit all the luggage at the homestead first.' Alick headed for the car immediately they emerged into the sunshine again.

'And we can stop and see Jim on the way. He'll know where Court is, for sure. Just follow that turn-off to the right.' He pointed to where the track through the complex diverged.

On backing out from beneath the tree, Eden complied with his directions. 'Who's Jim?' she enquired.

'Jim Stanley, the station's mechanic-cum-general handyman. If anything breaks down, he's the one who fixes it, and unless I'm very much mistaken we'll find him around the generator shed. The generators are his pride and joy, and he's always fussing over them. Of course, in view of the fact that, as a service for the guests, they're run continuously, day and night, it's probably just as well that he does,' he added with a graphic half-laugh.

'Mmm, I can imagine that with this number of people around it could be inconvenient, to say the least, if you suddenly lost all power.'

'Isn't that the truth!' he endorsed, and gestured for her to pull up in front of the appropriate building.

Just as Alick had predicted, they discovered that Court was indeed absent for the time being. From the property altogether, as it so happened, in fact, since that morning he had taken a group of visitors down to the old goldmining areas of Croydon and Golden Gate in order to inspect the now abandoned mines as well as to do a spot of fossicking, and that he wasn't expected to return before nightfall.

Disappointed though she was at being unable to have the matter of her employment settled immediately, Eden did her best to suppress any misgivings she felt regarding the situation as Alick then proceeded to show the way to the homestead and, after mounting the stairs to the broad, insect-screened veranda above, led her past spacious and tropically furnished sitting and dining-rooms to an airy blue and cream decorated bedroom that opened on to the balcony.

'This do you?' he enquired lightly as he set her two cases at the foot of the quilted bed.

'Thank you. It's lovely,' she approved sincerely, depositing her large camera bag beside the rest of her luggage. Like the rest of the house the room was large and uncluttered, with expanses of cool, polished wooden floor and obviously expensive fittings. It was also far removed from the quarters she had expected to inhabit while on the station, and as a result of the present uncertainty regarding her position, she still couldn't help but speculate, 'You don't think your stepbrother might consider it an imposition my occupying a room here? I mean, it's evident none of the staff usually stay in the homestead, and. . .'

'Well, it's hardly your fault the staff quarters are apparently full,' Alick cut in with a shrug. 'And since the rest of the accommodation provided is for guests, where else could you be expected to be housed?'

'I don't know,' she had little option but to concede, even if not entirely convinced. She just didn't want to provide his stepbrother, no matter how inadvertently, with an added reason for resisting her employment.

'Then since that's settled, we can now do our grand tour of the place, if you like.'

'Yes, I would, very much,' Eden owned, doing her best to match his unconcerned mood. Since he did appear so sure of the eventual outcome, maybe she *was* worrying for nothing. 'It could even stand me in good stead if I knew at least something of the set-up here before actually meeting your stepbrother.'

'Now you're on the right track,' commended Alick,
and with an arm about her shoulders began ushering
her downstairs again.

The rest of the afternoon proved a most interesting and informative one for Eden as her companion
pointed out the various staff quarters, the purposes
of the many outbuildings, and the self-contained
lodge accommodation for those visitors who either
flew in, or were seeking a little more comfort than
camping in the neat, tree-shaded area that had been
set aside for this purpose.

He also explained that, with the station being situated on one of the two arms of the Arrunga River,
the lure that brought many people to stay was the
succulent, fighting barramundi that were so abun-
dant in the property's almost two hundred miles of
both fresh and tidal waterways.

Then, of course, there were also the normal day-
to-day activities of a vast cattle station to be witnessed, together with sightseeing tours, wildlife
safaris, camp-out trail rides, and aircraft musters to
participate in. Dinghies with outboards were also
available for exploring the creeks and rivers, and sce-
nic flights made, especially over those areas of the
Gulf where meandering rivers wound their way
across tidal salt flats, creating intricate green-edged
patterns along their lengths as they lethargically
made their way to the sea.

As well, it was a naturalist's and a photographer's
paradise, she discovered, for the area teemed with
bird and animal life, a few tamed species of which—
including wallabies, emus, brolgas, and even a large
monitor lizard—wandered at will among the visitors.

When she returned to the homestead some hours later in order to prepare for dinner, however, all Eden's previous apprehensions quickly came racing back after meeting Alick's young half-brother, Joel— a tall, blond-headed young man who possessed an open, ready smile and was a couple of years older than herself. It was a somewhat confusing relationship that existed within their family, she knew, Joel being the product of the marriage of Alick's father to Court's mother. But it was the younger man's half amused, half wryly disbelieving reaction to his relative's explanation for her presence that disturbed her. Not that he showed any objections to the idea. He merely appeared to find the situation cause for enigmatic humour—much to Eden's disquiet.

In consequence, as she and Alick made their way across to the restaurant a short while later—more often than not the family had their meals there, she had learned, since there seemed little point in doing otherwise when the restaurant was open every day for the benefit of those campers, or other visitors, who felt like a rest from preparing their own meals—she put forward musingly, 'Joel didn't sound particularly encouraging, did he?'

'Oh, I don't know about that,' Alick dismissed on an insouciant note. 'More significantly, perhaps, he did agree that Court needed assistance, though, if you recall.'

Yes, he had done that, she had to concede. 'Provided your stepbrother is also prepared to own as much!'

'You worry too much.' Her consternation was, once again, rejected with a confidence she found extremely difficult to share, but as they had now reached the restaurant building it wasn't a matter she could dwell on at length.

When they entered, it was to find the bar filled with people, talking and laughing and discussing their various activities of the day. Some, dressed a little more formally than most, were obviously guests from the lodge accommodation. Others were just as evidently campers, a number of the staff—helicopter mustering pilots, or drivers as they were called, and ringers for the most part—among them also. But as yet there was still no sign of Alick's stepbrother.

In fact, it wasn't until they had concluded their meal in the strikingly furnished red and black dining-room, for which they had been joined by Joel and the station's overseer, plus two of the mustering pilots, and had repaired to the bar for a drink afterwards, that there was any indication of the return of Arrunga River's owner.

The first intimation came as a group of voluble, laughing people entered the room and promptly began to regale the two girls serving there—although to a somewhat reduced number of patrons now since most of the earlier crowd were either making use of the dining-room, or had returned to the camping area in order to prepare their own meals—with the happenings of their obviously enjoyable day.

'Court's back,' said Joel, sending a cryptic look across the table in his half-brother's direction.

'So I see,' Alick replied in wry accents, holding his gaze imperturbably.

Eden missed the little by-play altogether. From the moment Joel spoke, her anxious glance had been fixed on the new group milling about the bar in an effort to catch sight of and perhaps manage to obtain some insight as to the character of the man who had the final, and only, say regarding her employment on the property.

Suddenly her eyes came to rest on one particular male figure as Crystal hurried to speak to him, and somehow Eden knew she had located who she had been searching for—even without Crystal's sugary-sweet attitude to confirm her deduction.

He was tall, wide of shoulder, very muscular, and around thirty-two years old, she noted immediately. But that was as far as her assessment had time to proceed, because her attention was abruptly broken by Alick muttering a totally uncustomary, and unexpected, epithet under his breath.

'Damn and blast that bloody Crystal!' he continued in the same muted but livid manner. 'She's had her say to him about it already! I should have realised she would!' With his expression tightening in self-disgust he began swiftly rising to his feet. 'Come on, sweetie! I can see it's time we got to work on him. . . before *she* manages to do any more damage!'

Dismayed by his words, Eden hurried to do as directed and gained her own feet, her tawny eyes swinging back rapidly towards the bar, and promptly connecting with a slightly narrowed, sardonic gaze from the man there as he turned at that moment to look their way. It was a glance that had her colouring involuntarily, even as a small frown of puzzlement began drawing her winged brows together.

In view of Alick's surmise, she could have understood his stepbrother looking annoyed perhaps, but. . . sardonic? She shook her head perplexedly, unable to think of a reason for such a reaction, but knowing she hadn't been mistaken in reading his expression when it was succeeded by an equally explicit gesture with his head indicating for Alick to follow him as he swivelled on his heel and headed out of the bar area and into the office.

It just didn't seem to make sense, Eden continued to frown musingly as she trailed the pair of them into the room she and Alick had passed earlier in the afternoon, and absently took the seat he now offered her in front of a heavy wooden desk, the top of which was only just visible in places due to the amount of papers, books and letters strewn haphazardly across it. Nevertheless, under cover of the men's greetings—cordially, if a trifle ironically voiced—she made use of the opportunity to take further stock of the slightly younger man covertly.

Now that he had removed his bush hat she could see that his short-cropped hair was night dark and thick, his eyes a magnetic blue-green and ringed by long black lashes. He also possessed an attractively shaped, frankly sexy mouth, she decided contemplatively, his straight white teeth contrasting starkly against the dark tan of his skin. His jaw was lean, the faint cleft in its firm centre signalling an unmistakable tenacity that, in consequence, had her releasing a rather despondent sigh. Under the circumstances, such a trait didn't precisely augur well for him to change his mind regarding hiring an assistant.

'Hey, get with it, Eden! I've just been introducing you and Court,' Alick's expressive voice suddenly interrupted her thoughts, and for the second time in almost as many minutes she was unable to control her colour as she looked across the desk to where Court was now seated.

'I—I'm sorry,' she stammered self-consciously. 'I was just. . .' She halted quickly, biting her lip on

realising that her previous musings definitely weren't
meant for revealing. 'H-how do you do?' she just
managed to force out instead, albeit somewhat
lamely.

Court dipped his head imperceptibly in acknowledgement, his expression a mixture of irony,
impassivity, and just plain uninterest, and her feelings plummeted. Now he probably thought her
vacuous! she railed at herself angrily.

'And don't forget he's a Buchanan, not a Seaton,'
put in Alick drily, evidently deducing quite correctly
that she hadn't heard a word of his introduction.

'What?' She stared at him blankly for a second or
two. 'Oh, yes, of course,' she pushed out with a half-
smile, recovering, although not before her emotions
had taken an even further dive. What on earth was
she trying to do. . . sabotage herself? In an effort to
undo at least some of the damage, she made herself
face the man across the desk as steadily as possible.
'Please let me compliment you on the set-up you have
here, Mr—er—Buchanan. It's quite beautiful.'

He merely gave another of those faint tilts of his
dark head. 'Thank you. We're certainly happy with
the way it's developed to date.'

Implying that he had no intention of changing the
status quo, including the staffing levels? pondered
Eden dispiritedly.

'And it's Court, not Mr Buchanan,' inserted Alick
with a wry twist to his lips. 'No one ever calls him
anything else round here.' Pausing, he perched himself on a corner of the desk and cast his stepbrother
a bantering look as he gave a pseudo-deferential
salute. 'Except "boss" of course.'

Court's return gaze was mocking. 'Then maybe
you should have remembered that before you decided

to offer a reward that's neither available, nor yours
to give.'

Eden's forehead immediately furrowed once more.
Reward? For what? And why should he think Alick
would offer her one, anyway?

'Except that, in this case, I figure it's *you* I'm
rewarding,' countered Alick.

'Again?' Court quirked a satiric brow expressively
high.

The comment was ignored, by his stepbrother at
least. 'Because while Simone and Wade are away on
their overseas trip. . .' he turned to Eden to advise
for her benefit, 'that's his mother, my father, and
whose supposed four-month trip has now lasted for
ten months, with still no indication as to when it
might finally be concluded!' his glance was directed
to the other side of the desk again, '...it stands to reason you can't continue doing everything yourself—
despite your apparent reluctance to admit it! And, I
might add, Joel and the rest of the fellers we had dinner with evidently agree with me.'

Court flicked a cynical glance in Eden's direction
briefly before returning his attention to Alick.
'Golden girl already got them spellbound too, has
she?'

Both his tone and his words had Eden bristling,
and from having sat silently and allowing Alick to do
the talking, she now angled her chin higher and spoke
up in her own defence. 'No, they weren't spellbound!' she denied with some asperity. 'They could
apparently just see the sense of providing you with
an assistant!'

'Mmm. . . and Alick just happened to find you
out of the blue, I suppose,' he put forward as ironically as ever.

'N-no,' she faltered, her emotions subsiding a little as she wondered just what he was getting at. 'As a matter of fact, we've known each other for just over two years now. We happened to work in the same building.'

Court's lips shaped crookedly as he slanted his stepbrother a wry gaze. 'That must have been. . . convenient.'

'You should know,' Alick grinned chaffingly. 'After all, it's been the solicitors Eden worked for that I've sought advice from on your behalf in the past.'

Court nodded slowly. 'Ah, a legal firm.' His eyes held his relative's steadily. 'So suitable for providing a relevant grounding in the tourist industry.'

'Dealing with the public is much the same no matter which industry's involved.' Eden decided it was time for her to have another say in the matter, but carefully disregarded her own doubts experienced only a few hours earlier on just the same point.

'A consideration that is neither here nor there, I might point out, when a vacancy just doesn't exist,' Court had no compunction in declaring on a rather more resolute note.

'Except that, in this case, there are evidently a number of others here, beside myself, who obviously believe there should be,' put in Alick quickly. He paused, his expression becoming persuasive. 'And in view of the fact that Eden has already resigned from her previous position, not to mention her having driven all the way out here. . .' He raised an expressive shoulder.

In return, Court's own features assumed a decidedly sardonic cast. 'None of which would have occurred if you'd merely confined yourself to hiring the photographer I *did* request you to employ!'

'Oh, but that was the beauty of the whole idea, you see,' Alick advised blithely. 'Because Eden's your photographer as well, so you'll be getting two for the price of one, so to speak.'

Court's shapely mouth levelled noticeably. 'Except that I was only interested in employing one! And professional photography being just another of those—er—accomplishments she managed to pick up while typing wills, I presume?'

The inherent sarcasm in his last contention had Eden sucking in a resentful breath and sending a stormy glance across the desk. 'No, I didn't just *pick it up*,' gratingly stressed, 'while I was at work! It's been a hobby of mine for a great many years, and one which I happen to have put a lot of effort and money into, I might add! I admit that still doesn't make me a professional, but at the same time I have won a number of amateur competitions *and* sold quite a few photographs to travel bureaux and the like, so I'm damned if I'm going to meekly accept you denigrating my work simply because you object to Alick having offered me a position here! I don't want any job *that* badly!' she scorned, eyes sparkling. 'So if you'll excuse me. . .' Pushing out of her chair, she turned for the door, only slowing long enough to counsel heavily, 'You're wasting your time, Alick. There's no way you're going to convince *him* to even accept an assistant, let alone *me* in that role!'

'No, you're wrong, sweetie! There's plenty more to be said yet,' Alick began urgently, but with a repudiating shake of her head Eden continued on her way. Behind her, she heard him remonstrate, 'Damn it, Court, why did you have to take it out on her? I'm the one your quarrel's with!'

What his stepbrother had to say in reply to that, Eden didn't stop to hear, didn't even want to hear. She just kept walking, aimlessly for a while, and then down to the deserted beach eventually, where she sank down on to the sand with her back against a tall palm, and cupping her face in her hands as she rested her elbows on her updrawn knees, stared mistily out across the moonlit sea.

It was hard to believe that it had been only the day before that she had set out from Townsville with such eagerness, looking forward to just such an opportunity to sit on the sands beneath a silvery Carpentaria moon, or that even as recently as that very afternoon she had been so delighted to think she would be working in such glorious surroundings, she brooded dejectedly. There was no hope of that ever occurring now, of course. She knew it, even if Alick might still be refusing to admit defeat. With a dismal sigh, she wiped the back of her hand across her damp lashes and extracted a cigarette from the packet in her purse.

She was still there a couple of hours and a number of cigarettes later when, from along the beach, Alick came stumbling towards her.

'So this is where you got to,' he said wryly, dropping down beside her and gratefully removing his sand-filled shoes. Just as she had done earlier. 'I've been looking for you everywhere.'

In order to tell her what she had already worked out for herself, she supposed. 'I'm sorry. So what time will we be leaving tomorrow?'

'Well, I'll be leaving on the afternoon mail plane, as arranged.' He paused, his eyes crinkling at the corners. 'While you. . . will be remaining here.'

Eden stared at him blankly. 'I will?'

'Uh-huh!' he grinned. 'I told you to leave everything to your Uncle Alick, didn't I? Well, Court's finally agreed to give it a trial.'

Earlier Eden would have been elated at such news, but now it only engendered a faint surprise. 'Because you eventually managed to wear him down, or because you succeeded in making him feel obliged to give me a go?' she hazarded sceptically.

'Does it matter?'

'Well, of course it does! I couldn't stay here knowing that I really wasn't wanted.'

'Then I guess it would be up to you to prove him wrong, wouldn't it?'

'How do you mean?'

'Oh, come on, Eden, you can do better than that!' he reproved. 'How do you think I mean? By making a success of the position, naturally! Because, you heard the others, he *does* need an assistant!' Suddenly he tilted her face up to his, surveying her doubtful expression watchfully. 'Or have you now changed your mind?'

Eden hunched diffidently away from the question. 'I—I'm not sure,' she confessed honestly, and sighed. 'I was looking forward to it very much, but with your stepbrother apparently more or less only suffering my presence, it's not exactly an inviting, or encouraging, situation to contemplate.'

'Although the remedy *is* in your hands.'

She bit her lip pensively. 'Do you really think so, Alick? I mean. . . honestly?'

He both smiled and nodded. 'Uh-huh, honestly. If anyone could, I reckon you can. And you'll never know unless you give it a try.'

'No, I guess not,' she allowed, feeling herself wanting to be convinced. 'And I could always leave later, if—if it didn't work out, I suppose.'

'There's always that option,' he agreed. 'So what's it to be? Have I arranged it all for nothing, or. . .?' He raised an expressive brow.

Eden drew a deep breath. 'No, I'll give it a go. That is what I came for, after all, and even if the position is apparently only temporary, at best,' she half smiled tremulously.

'What makes you think that?' Alick frowned.

She lifted a deprecating shoulder. 'Well, in the office you did more or less imply that it would only be while your stepmother and father are away.'

'Oh, that!' He smiled his comprehension. 'Yes, well, I guess that could all depend on what you term temporary,' he advised in whimsical tones. 'Because not only is there no indication of them returning as yet, but from the tone of their last communication, I wouldn't be at all surprised if, once they do come home, it's only for a short time in order to catch up on what's been happening here before they set off for somewhere else. In which case "temporary" could be some considerable time. . . and the main reason for my having involved myself in the station's affairs and offered you a job here.'

Eden slanted him a speaking look. 'Even if you weren't entitled to offer any such thing!' Then, curiously, 'But don't you mind not having a say? I mean, I know you used to live here, and since you're also older than Court. . .'

'Mmm, but he's still the actual owner of the property. After all, it did belong to *his* father when he was alive, and his grandfather before that, etcetera. While

as to not really having a say. . . well, that's not
strictly correct, really. If you can put up a logical,
feasible argument concerning the running of the station, Court will always consider it, at least. As I would
have thought I'd just proved!' He tapped her lightly
beneath the chin to laughingly emphasise the point,
and had her spirits rising a little in response. Maybe
he would be proved right, after all.

'So that had nothing to do with you leaving
Arrunga River and living in Townsville instead,
then?'

'Lord, no! I just prefer the life, and the—er—
attractions to be found in the city, that's all.'

'By that you mean *female* attractions, of course,'
Eden charged drily.

'Are there any other kind?' he countered with an
unabashed grin.

'Not that you've had time to discover, I'm sure!'
she retorted with a half-laugh as, by tacit agreement,
they prepared to return to the homestead.

CHAPTER TWO

THE FIRST faint streaks of light were only just beginning to chase away the dark when a pounding on her door awakened Eden the following morning, and still feeling half asleep, she scrambled out of bed to throw on a wrapper before stumbling across the barely lit room to answer the imperative summons.

'Sorry to wake you, my sweet, and I know it's an ungodly hour, but if you're wanting to come to grips with this new job of yours then I suggest you get yourself across to the airstrip right now!' recommended Alick urgently as soon as she had flung open the door.

'The airstrip?' Eden repeated bewilderedly, combing her fingers through her tousled hair, and still not fully awake.

'Uh-huh! Because that muted roar you can hear is the choppers warming up, and since I've just discovered Court and Joel have already left the house, I suspect they're going out on today's muster too,' he elucidated swiftly. 'And that being the case, I figure you've got about five minutes to get over there before Court disappears for the remainder of the day. . . and you're conveniently left without any acknowledgement or instructions concerning your position here!'

It didn't make sense to Eden. 'But I thought you said last night that he'd agreed to give me a trial!'

'So he did. However, I didn't also say that meant he would be volunteering any information regarding it, though, did I?'

'But—but surely, in that case. . .'

'For God's sake, Eden, you're just wasting time!' Alick cut her off peremptorily. 'Save the questions for later! *Now* is the time for action in order to pin him down on the matter!'

'Okay, okay!' She threw her hands up in the air in defeat, giving up trying to understand in favour of simply being guided.

He doubtless knew better than she did, anyway, and maybe her brain still wasn't functioning quite as quickly or as lucidly as it could either, she decided as she obediently raced through the motions of dressing, splashed some water over her face, and went racing off towards the airstrip as directed.

In the darkened, unfamiliar surroundings, Eden's path seemed littered with obstacles as she hurried past enclosures and around trees, once even being liberally doused with water from one of the many sprinklers that helped keep the environs of the complex so lush and green because she hadn't seen it to avoid it in the faint light.

Nevertheless, on approaching the gateway that led on to the airstrip, she couldn't discern any figures between herself and the helicopters whose engines at that distance shattered the still morning air, and fearing Court might already have been aboard began to increase her pace. Although only until a hard hand abruptly gripped hold of her arm as she passed through the deep shadows created by a spreading tree beside the gateway and she was swung to a gasping, jolting halt, her momentum sending her cannoning into a tall male form.

'Where in hell do you think you're rushing off to at this hour?' promptly came the exasperated demand in a distinctively resonant voice. 'And keep still, damn you!' Both the fingers that hadn't yet released her and the tone tightened warningly.

Startled by the unexpectedness of her halt, and Court's appearance—not to mention his exasperated instruction—Eden did her best to recover her faculties, and her breath. 'I—I was trying to catch up with. . .' she started to explain, but came to a stop on discovering him to be paying not the slightest attention as he concentrated his gaze somewhere to the left of the helicopters. In lieu, she frowned curiously. 'What is it? Why are we having to stand here, anyway?'

Court inhaled deeply—irritatedly? Eden speculated—but didn't alter the direction of his glance. 'Because there's a couple of feral pigs on the other side of the strip.'

'But they'll disappear once the helicopters start to take off, won't they?'

'Or someone goes sprinting across there,' he confirmed with a decidedly satirical inflection.

Meaning herself, she presumed, and grimaced. 'Well, then?'

Now he did spare her a brief look. 'I'm waiting on Joel returning with a rifle to ensure they *don't* get the chance to disappear, because they happen to be noxious pests, and until the choppers started warming up they were on this side of the strip destroying great expanses of the lawns by devouring the roots,' she was informed succinctly.

'Oh!' Eden shrugged defensively. So how was she supposed to have known that? 'Well, now that you've explained the position, you don't have to keep holding on to me, you know. I can assure you I'm not about to begin leaping all over the place uttering banshee wails,' she retaliated with a little sarcasm of her own.

This time the look she received lasted somewhat longer. Discomfitingly longer as it ranged over her dissectingly, and the hand that had been holding her was, along with his other, dropped to rest on lean hips. 'And if you're dissatisfied with matters here, you have the perfect solution, don't you?'

There was no mistaking his implication and Eden swallowed hard, recalling her reason for having followed him in the first place, although Joel's timely arrival with a heavy calibre rifle relieved her of the necessity of replying as Court's attention returned to more immediate concerns.

'G'day, Eden! What on earth are you doing here?' were the youngr man's first surprised words on reaching them.

'Good question!' inserted Court sardonically.

'Here! You're the better shot,' Joel grinned wryly, handing over the weapon, and without waiting for an answer from Eden to his greeting.

Not judging it the time to explain her presence, especially in view of Court's expressive comment, Eden hadn't actually intended to give more than a smile—albeit only a half one in this instance—in acknowledgement in any case.

'We're starting to get a few of them around again, aren't we?' Joel continued.

Court nodded as he moved closer to the fence. 'Mmm, it looks as if we'll have to arrange another shooting party shortly.' Then, drawing back the bolt on the rifle, he thrust it forward again to ram a cartridge into the breach, and took aim.

In quick succession he fired, reloaded, and fired again, the crack of the shots reverberating even above the noise of the helicopters, and among the shadows of the tree on the opposite side of the airstrip—barely distinguishable to Eden's untrained eyes—two black shapes crashed to the ground.

'Hey, that was good shooting in this light!' lauded Joel immediately. 'You got 'em both!'

An assessment Eden was very much in agreement with, but diffidence had her refraining from saying so.

'Well, they're both down, but whether they're both actually done for could be another matter,' Court qualified wryly. 'The second one was already turning away as I aimed and I may have only wounded it. We'd better check, just to be on the safe side.

Reloading once more in anticipation, he began heading through the gateway on to the strip with Joel beside him, but resolving not to be dismissed and left behind—purposely so, she suspected where Court was concerned—Eden resolutely followed, if a discreet distance.

They were almost to the other side when one of the animals did indeed suddenly stagger to its feet, but instead of setting off into the bush, it let out an infuriated half squeal, half grunt, and charged for the figures nearing it. It all happened so swiftly that Eden was unable to contain the involuntary gasp of surprise and alarm that rose in her throat, then promptly bit her lip in dismay on realising how it had distracted the two in front of her when, for a split second, both their heads automatically swung in her direction.

'For God's sake, get her away from here!' barked Court on a harsh note to his half-brother even as he started to take aim.

In a few swift strides Joel reached Eden's side and grabbing hold of her hand began dragging her unceremoniously along with him as he ran towards the nearest of the helicopters. 'Are you bloody mad? Why didn't you stay back on the other side? You don't take chances with wild pigs at any time, let alone when they might be wounded! You could get someone killed by distracting them at a moment like that!' he castigated roughly, taking a worried look backwards.

'I know. And I—I'm sorry, t-truly I am!' panted Eden, abashed, and stumbling a little as she also cast apprenhensiveeyes over her shoulder towards Court. God, she would never forgive herself if she was the cause of him being injured, or—or worse! Seeing how close the razor-toothed boar was to him had her breath catching fearfully in her throat, and then she jumped compulsively as another rapid two shots crashed out.

To her sagging relief the pig finally crumpled and lay still a mere yard or so from where Court was standing, and seeing it Joel also came to a stop, relinquishing his grip on her, and turned to retrace their steps at a more normal pace. Eden remained where she was on abruptly trembling legs, and watched while they satisfied themselves that neither beast would ever again present any more danger. This completed, they then made their way towards Eden, and she gulped nervously on observing the taut, forbidding expression on Court's features.

'Over here, honey!' He raised an imperatively beckoning forefinger as he changed direction slightly, veering back towards the complex, but didn't stop moving. 'You and I have some unfinished business to discuss, and I wouldn't want any misunderstandings to occur because of the noise *they're* making,' indicating the rotating blades of the helicopters not far distant.

Eden nodded jerkily, her stomach contricting, and made her way across to him with reluctant steps.

'In the meantime, I'll—er—return the rifle and arrange for the disposal of those carcasses,' put in Joel diplomatically, and taking the firearm set off swiftly for the homestead.

Somehow, Eden thought she might have preferred it if he had remained. She had no idea just how Court was likely to react, and Joel's presence could perhaps have been a restraining influence. As it was, when he didn't immediately speak on her reaching him, but merely quickened his determined stride, she impulsively decided to take the plunge herself.

'Look, I'm sorry, really sorry, for—for having diverted your attention at such a. . .'

'You shouldn't even have been there in the first place!' Court interrupted in rough-edged tones.

'It still wasn't my intention to put you in danger,' she defended contritely. 'I—I just didn't realise, that's all.'

'Precisely why you had not business being there! And in view of the fact that *I* had the rifle, and know something of the behaviour of feral pigs, *you* were probably the one in most danger, honey!' As he paused, his expression, quite visible now in the increasing light, took on a caustically mocking cast. 'And what would Alick have had to say if I'd allowed something to happened to you, hmm?'

Eden drew a vexed breath. Just what was he insinuating now? That she and Alick might have been more than just acquaintances? 'Considering the circumstances, he'd doubtlessly say I had no one to blame but myself! Not that he has any particular reason to make *any* comment, if it comes to that!' she added insistently in order to make the position clear. Then went on in a more conciliatory tone, 'I'm well aware it was my fault, and I apologise, but I only followed you because I was interested.'

'Then in future I suggest you restrict your interests, and preferably yourself, to the confines of the complex!'

'Well, at least it seemed she was still to *have* a future at Arrunga River, instead of receiving her marching orders as she had quite expected. And truthfully, his attitude had been far less demoralising than she had expected. None the less, to suggest she confine her activities to the complex Eden considered a little extreme, especially as it could only hamper her efforts to effectively fulfil her position as Tourist Manager. Or was that the whole idea? the sneaking suspicion soon followed. When all was said and done, and despite his apparent agreement with Alick to the contrary, he still hadn't exactly given any indication that he found the notion of an assistant acceptable.

'All because of one unthinking mistake?' she charged with a hint of resentment. 'You're just using it as an excuse to go back on your word!'

'Correction, honey!' Court's aquamarine eyes held hers intently. 'I *never* go back on my word, and around here nor do I need *excuses* for any of my decisions! So that's two things you'd better get straight, for a start!' Half turning, he raised a hand—to indicate he would be joining them shortly, Eden assumed—when Joel passed on his way out to the helicopters again. 'And now, if that's all, I'll be going.' He touched a finger to the wide brim of his hat and started to take his leave.

'No, that's not all!' Eden burst out hastily, and with some asperity. She wasn't going to allow him to evade the main issue that easily. 'You still haven't told me what work you want me to do. . . which *was* the reason for my rushing out here, after all!' A thread of sarcasm made its appearance.

'I did wonder about that,' he halted to drawl wryly. His eyes roved over her leisurely, his attractively shaped mouth beginning to twitch. 'And also about why you appear to be wearing wet clothes, if it come to that.'

Eden dropped her gaze self-consciously to her still damp shirt and lightweight jeans. Of course, she had to have run into the heaviest fall of the water, she derided, and of course, he did have to have noticed! Maybe it wasn't so surprising he thought she should remain within the immediate environs of the homestead. Right from their introduction she seemed to have done nothing but present herself as none too bright!

'I failed to see one of the sprinklers in the dark,' she disclosed at last in something of a mumble.

There was a brief silence, and then, 'Well, you certainly couldn't claim to have had an auspicious beginning to your day, could you?'

The lightly mocking humour she thought she detected in his voice only served to make Eden feel more discomfited, but in an attempt to prevent him from guessing just how much, she made herself lift

her head, her darkly lashed amber eyes holding his
determinedly. 'I guess not,' she allowed grudgingly.
She couldn't very well have said otherwise. 'Although
I'm sure that will all change once you *do* give me some
instructions as to the work I should undertake.'

'Hmm. . .' He paused meditatively, his lips curving crookedly, and again raised his hand in a brief
salute in the direction of the helicopters when, much
to Eden's surprise, they began lifting into the air.
'Take some photos,' he proposed laconically, and
prepared to head towards the fence.

'Some photos!' she echoed, taken aback. 'I meant,
work concerning tourist activities! And—and aren't
you taking part in the aerial muster today?'

'No, I'll be working down at the yards most of the
day. While as to the other—you also asked for my
instructions, and. . .,' he slanted her an eloquent
glance over a broad shoulder, 'Alick did say it was
two for the price of one, remember? *Photographs!*' he
repeated succinctly with an emphasising nod, and
continued on his way.

This time Eden didn't comment, speculating that
there had been enough implacability in that last
direction to signal that she would simply be wasting
her time, but she expelled a disgruntled breath instead
as she watched him leave. Court Buchanan might
have agreed to give her a trial, but at the same it was
rapidly becoming more than plain that he wasn't
about to do so too readily!

'So how did you go?' Alick asked interestedly as soon
as Eden returned to the homestead. 'I heard the
shots—presumably there were a couple of pigs
around, there was talk about them at dinner last

night—and gathered the delay must have enabled you to catch up with Court before he left.'

'Except that he didn't leave at all, but will apparently be working in the yards today,' Eden advised with a grimace, dropping into a chair on the verandah. 'And as for how I went. . .' she hunched a slender shoulder expressively, 'well, let's put it this way. Which would you rather hear first? The good news, or the bad news?'

'Like that, is it?' He uttered a wry half-laugh. 'I think you'd better hit me with the good news first, then.'

'Yes, well, the good news is. . . I didn't actually manage to get him killed,' she relayed in self-mocking tones.

Momentarily, Alick looked a trifle stunned, and then he recovered sufficiently to nod slowly. 'Mmm, I guess that certainly would be classified as good news,' he confirmed somewhat ironically. 'Although I think I'd prefer to digest that information a little longer before seeking an explanation, if you don't mind. So tell me, what's the bad news?' He fixed her with a decidedly askance gaze.

'The bad news is. . . that I strongly surmise he's going to fight every inch of the way against allowing me to take over *any* of his responsibilities!' She made a sardonic moue. 'Which, perhaps, is understandable, seeing he undoubtedly considers me totally brainless!'

He shook his head in confused disbelief, and obviously unable to decide whether to smile or frown. 'What in hell happened out there?' he enquired dazedly.

'You're positive you really want to know?'

'At the moment I'm not sure about anything, but I think maybe I'd better if I'm to understand any of it.'

'In that case. . .' Eden shrugged and proceeded to divulge—in satirical tones mostly, directed against herself—the relevant details.

'Oh, well, that's not too bad. Initially, I thought it was going to be a lot worse,' Alick asserted with a relieved smile when she had finished. 'It's mainly only minor mishaps that could have happened to anyone, and it was evidently only a *suggestion* that you confine yourself to the complex,' with a sly grin. 'While as for Court's attitude—well, I must admit I had suspicions myself that there was still some reluctance there to accept the situation entirely.' He went on quickly, buoyantly, 'However, I'm sure you'll have no difficulty in overcoming that temporary obstacle in no time at all.'

Eden wasn't anywhere near as certain and shook her head ruefully, never failing to be amazed by his blithe dismissal of every problem. 'And meanwhile, since he's apparently not about to say, perhaps *you'd* care to suggest just how I'm to go about discovering exactly how, and in which areas, I'm to provide him with assistance.' She pulled a drily explicit face. 'Ask Crystal, maybe?'

Alick responded with a caustic snort. 'That would be on a par with a moth asking the spider for help to escape its web! No, at a guess I'd say you would probably be best asking Gaye Redman—the blonde girl who was also serving in the bar last night—anything you want to know concerning tourist activities and so forth. It's likely she would have as good an idea as anyone—apart from Joel, of course, when he's around.' Pausing, he shrugged an insouciant shoulder. 'Not that you need worry about any of that today, in any event, since Court's instructed you to take some photos instead. Because you were keen to have a go at preparing the brochure, weren't you?'

'Very,' she was only too willing to admit, albeit with a proviso. 'Although only in addition to my other supposed work—not in place of it! I mean, today I was expecting to find out how the tourist arrangements are made, and where, around here. Moreover, just where am I to work from—if I'm ever to be permitted to, that is—for a start? The office, the bar, the homestead, or is it literally a roving commission?'

Alick shrugged. 'Probably the latter, I guess. At least, I think that's how Simone and Wade used to do it, by simply being on hand most of the time. And I expect that's more or less how Court's been operating too. . . when he's available. Naturally enough, he can't devote all his time to the visitors, because primarily it's still a cattle station he's running. They have to fit in with the daily operations of the property, so he wouldn't have had the time to be waiting around in an office, or some such, for people to approach him. They'd have just had to collar hold of him whenever they saw him.'

'Which could make it somewhat difficult for me to become established in the position if he doesn't intend—as seems quite possible—advising anyone that they should now direct any such enquiries to me. They'll all automatically continue to seek him out for any information they need,' Eden reasoned with a sigh. An oblique tilt began pulling at her mobile mouth. 'And that's quite apart from me not having been provided with any precise details concerning the attractions available, or even the information necessary to enable me to answer any general questions regarding the station itself, if it comes to that!'

'Oh, well, I could perhaps help you there to some degree, and give you something of a brief tour of the immediate surroundings, at least, while you take some of those photos,' he offered helpfully. 'It might also be an opportune time for you to get some shots down at the yards if, as you say, they're working there today. . . *and* maybe get some of the information you're after from Court, since there are usually a few spectators around when there's cattle in the yards, which would make it somewhat difficult for him to ignore or evade any questions you might ask,' with another wily smile. 'As well, there are bound to be some of the old brochures, mud maps, etcetera, in the office that could be helpful with specific details. We could collect some after breakfast. And talking of breakfast. . .,' he grinned and began rising to his feet, 'I reckon I could do with some right about now. How about you?'

'I wouldn't say no,' she half laughed, her spirits lifting at the prospect of being able to learn *something* that might help insinuate herself into her new position. 'I've been out of bed so long it feels like the middle of the morning already. I'd better have a proper wash first, though.' She executed an eloquent grimace on gaining her own feet. 'I didn't exactly have time to do so when you woke me.' Her shirt and jeans she decided she might as well continue wearing, since they were almost dry again now.

CHAPTER THREE

AN HOUR or so later, their meal concluded, and armed with an assortment of advertising material from the office, as well as a roughly sketched map outlining those areas and waterways nearest the homestead complex, Eden collected her large camera bag which she slung over her shoulder and, together with Alick, made her way down to the large and intricate set of solid wooden yards situated some distance away where a massive road train—made up of a diesel-powered prime mover coupled to three long double-decker trailers—stood ready beside the loading ramp.

Inside the yards there were a couple of hundred head of cattle of differing sizes being drafted. Some to be turned off to the saleyards; the rest to be dipped and the younger ones, the cleanskins, branded; but all of them stamping around so restlessly that clouds of dust floated high into the air.

As Alick had forecast, there were also a number of other interested onlookers present, most carrying cameras and busily clicking away as Court and the three ringers with him—not to mention the energetic and knowing blue-speckled cattle dogs—went about their work efficiently and with a speed borne of long practice.

For a time Eden didn't set to work with her own camera, though, but studied the scene speculatively, looking for the best angles, the best backgrounds, and the areas of bright sunlight and strong shade that could so easily trap the unwary photographer.

'Aren't you going to take any photos, then? Don't you consider the scene good enough?' Alick enquired after a while when she still hadn't made any move to take her camera from the bag.

Eden nodded quickly. 'Oh, yes, it's great! It's just that. . . would it be possible to get a little closer, do you think?' She eyed him hopefully.

'Inside, you mean? Where the branding fire is?'

'Well, that would certainly be best of all, but. . .' her expression turned a little wry, 'perhaps Court might have something to say about that.'

Alick shrugged. 'I don't see why. When all's said and done, it was his idea that you take photographs today, and that being so, I guess that also designates you as official photographer. . . which should give you entrance to wherever you want to go,' he contended with a smile and, cupping her elbow in his hand, started them for the gate leading into the yards.

Eden was certain Court hadn't intended to designate her official anything, but made no demur all the same. The empty pen where the branding fire was located, being central to the holding yards, the race leading to the crush where the calves were being branded, and the dip, was the best vantage point as far as taking photos was concerned, after all.

When they entered the middle pen, Court was just shutting the gate after the most recent group of steers had been drafted into the loading yard, but on seeing them he climbed back through the rails, his expression hidden in the shadows created by the brim of his hat as he moved towards them with an easy, supple stride.

'Come to offer your services, have you?' he enquired of Alick in a lazy drawl as he reached them.

'Not me, old son,' his stepbrother discounted with a wry laugh. 'No, I'm only here to lend Eden a hand while she takes some photos.'

Court nodded slowly and flicked an oblique look in the girl's direction. 'Well, try not to fall in the dip, or something similar, and make sure you keep out of everyone's way, huh?'

Eden flushed, smarting under the obvious, if indirect, reference to her earlier mishaps. 'I wouldn't dream of doing otherwise!' she gritted in somewhat gibing accents. 'Unless, of course, you'd prefer me to photograph the yards later. . . when they're empty!' She arched a delicate brow.

'With your record to date, it could be safer for all concerned at that!' he showed no aversion to retorting, and giving a mocking tug on the brim of his hat turned on his heel in response to a call from one of the ringers and made his way over to the crush.

Eden heaved a disgruntled breath and cast a rueful glance at the man beside her. 'Well, have I managed to get myself banished, or not?' she grimaced.

'Oh, of course not!' Alick denied with a smile. 'You're reading far too much into what he says, that's all.' A sentiment she found extremely difficult to accept. 'Now where do you want to start? With the branding, the mob in the holding yard, the dip. . .?'

'Um. . . the mob in the yard, I guess. Before they're all drafted into separate pens,' she decided and scanning the area quickly, settled on a large shady tree some distance away as the safest place to set her bag down before beginning to get to work.

Presently, once she was satisfied with the coverage she had obtained of those particular cattle, Eden next headed for the roofed dip where, after proceeding through the race and the crush, the cattle had to plunge into the deep but narrow waterway in order to reach the ramp leading into the open yard on the other side.

'What are they being dipped for, Court?' called one of the visitors across the yard, and reminding Eden of Alick's suggestion that it could be a good opportunity for her to also make some enquiries.

'Buffalo fly,' came the answer, accompanied by the clanging of steel as the gates were opened to allow a cow through the crush and then swiftly pushed shut again in order to hold fast the calf behind her.

'Don't you throw them to brand them any more?' asked somebody else.

'At the yards out in the bush we often do, but not when there's a crush available,' Court supplied.

'Mmm, I guess it must be a lot easier this way,' the man nodded, and brought a wryly confirming smile to the face of the ringer testing the heat of one of the three branding irons in the fire.

Moving back towards the fire herself now, Eden made the most of the short lull that followed to find out what she wanted to know also. 'And the camp-out trail rides mentioned in your advertising literature, how long are they for?' she questioned with feigned casualness.

A nonchalance Court still had no difficulty seeing through, it appeared, for he immediately fixed her with an ironically knowing gaze. 'That's quite a change in subject, isn't it?' he murmured in a mocking undertone as he released the now branded calf and it scurried towards the dip. 'I thought it was branding and dipping that were being discussed.'

Evading his decidedly disconcerting glance, she shrugged with creditable insouciance and deliberately raised her voice to a level so that everyone could hear. 'Oh, but I'm sure there must be others here who would be interested to learn more about trail rides too.'

'Trail rides?' a male voice amongst the spectators immediately picked up in obviously interested tones—much to Eden's gratitude. 'As a matter of fact, I've been meaning to ask a few questions about those myself.'

Eden could have hugged him, whoever he was, and in her delight she dared to cast her employer a openly chaffing smile. 'And what better place to start than to discover how long they're for?' she put forward, tongue-in-cheek, and promptly felt a nervous tingle make its way down her spine in response to the considering glint that filtered into his dusky-lashed eyes.

'Then, normally, they're for either two or four days,' he at last provided the information she wanted, although she did note, vexedly, that it was directed towards the male visitor rather than herself, all the same.

It was Eden, though, who made certain she did most of the questioning. 'The four-day one being for more experienced riders?' she hazarded.

'Not necessarily, although it could prove to be slightly—er—uncomfortable for those who haven't done any riding for some time,' he drawled explicitly as two more cows were allowed through to the dip unimpeded before the gates were shut again on another calf.

Eden nodded, grimacing inwardly in understanding, and doing her best to remember everything for her own future reference. 'And since I presume they need a guide, who goes with them. . . you?'

He shook his head and moved to retrieve another of the irons from the fire. 'Not usually, no. Most times it's a couple of the ringers who not only know the property well, but among other things, are also capable of using a camp oven for cooking.'

'I see.' She paused as a puff of smoke rose from the calf's rump and the smell of burning hair pervaded the air, trying to think what other information might be of use to her. 'Do they always follow the same route?' she queried at length when the branding iron had once again been set to reheating.

'On occasion. It depends on the time of year to some degree, and the things of interest those concerned wish to see,' Court relayed in somewhat less impassive tones, adding on a lowered but caustic note, 'Aren't you supposed to be taking photographs?'

'I was just about to continue doing so,' Eden declared, if not altogether truthfully. None the less, prudently deducing that she, at least, had probably done as well as she was going to for the moment, she did make for the race with the intention of taking a few shots of the cattle moving through it.

This immediately proved rather less successful than she had envisaged, because whereas the cattle had until then been passing along it, if not precisely willingly, then at least with only a few persuading whacks of his hat by the ringer working the gate leading into it, they now began to display an almost mule-like refusal to take another step. In fact, the leading beast even managed to get itself hopelessly stuck sideways between the rails in its sudden efforts to turn around and head in the opposite direction.

Its alarming bellowing at finding itself in such a predicament soon had those following it jostling each other frantically as well as they, in turn, also attempted to turn back on those pushing from behind, and for a time disorder reigned until Court and the other men, along with much snapping and barking from the dogs, finally succeeded in extricating the trapped animal and had them all moving forward in more or less orderly fashion once more.

'How about you try doing as you're told. . . and keep out of the way, hmm?' Court suggested with noticeable corrosiveness as he passed her on his way back to the crush.

Eden's topaz-coloured eyes widened in surprise, then sparkled with indignation as she glared after him. She hadn't *been* in the way! How could she have when she hadn't even been within ten feet of either the cattle or the men as they worked to clear them? He was simply using it as an excuse to find fault! she decided, and threw him another acrimonious glare before stepping towards the race once more.

No sooner had she done so, however, than the leading beast immediately propped in the same fashion the last one had, those following pushing against each other nervously and trying to turn in an effort to back up but prevented from doing so by those coming behind, and making it necessary for the men to leave what they were doing in order to sort them out again.

'Why are they suddenly doing that, Court?' quizzed a voice from outside the yards.

'Because they're very wary of humans. . . especially when they're approached head-on!' he advised, the latter on a somewhat roughened note as he neared Eden and, grasping her about the waist with hard hands, moved her bodily to one side. Then, eyeing her exasperatedly, 'For God's sake, can't you see that it's *you* who's making them so damned agitated?'

'Me?' she gasped incredulously. 'But I'm nowhere near them!'

'Evidently they consider otherwise! And why in hell do you think I told you to keep out of the way last time, then?'

'Since you didn't see fit to offer any explanation, I had no idea!' she defended, not a little resentfully. 'How was I to know they're that jumpy?'

'By noting their reaction to your movements, I would have thought!' Court retorted in heavily sardonic tones.

Eden drew a nettled breath. 'Then if I'm not allowed to approach them from the front in order to photograph them, perhaps you'd care to tell me just how I am supposed to get within range!' A satiric note entered her own voice.

'Why not try—from the rear! The same as the rest of us do!'

'But I'm not interested in photographing a load of rumps!'

'That's as may be, but you'll still approach them that way in future. . . or else!' he warned, no trace of relieving sarcasm evident now, and continued on to the race before she could say anything more.

Eden pressed her lips together mutinously and grimaced at his departing back. Then her eyes sought out Alick to see if he might have some helpful advice to impart, but only to find him still beneath the tree where she had deposited her camera bag, and apparently deep in conversation with a couple of camera-laden tourists on the opposite side of the rails. Sighing on realising little aid was likely to be forthcoming from that direction, she turned back to discover the men returning to their previous positions and the cattle steadily moving forward again.

'I'm sorry for apparently having created extra work for you,' she apologised quietly to the youngest of the three ringers as he passed.

He grinned and shrugged unconcernedly. 'No worries. . . it happens. I've done it myself before now—as has just about everyone else some time or another. They're just not used to being handled very often, that's all.'

'I see,' she smiled back, grateful for his understanding. If someone else could also have taken the time to explain in the first place, the whole episode would probably have been avoided. 'I just didn't realise.'

'No, well, I guess. . .'

'Get a move on, Ross! We're just about ready for the next batch!' A call from Court in long-suffering accents suddenly intervened. 'Golden girl's supposed to be photographing the action. . . not providing a distraction!'

With a rueful smile and a dip of his head, Ross made his way back to his station on one of the gates, leaving Eden to control as best she could not only her embarrassment, but also her flaring resentment at her employer's purposely exaggerated tone—at least in her estimation—his unwarranted contention regarding her stopping Ross from working, and last though by no means least, his annoying use of that somehow insinuating nickname.

In the process of subduing her rebellious emotions she also resolved on a little retaliation in the form of more questions—whether he liked it or not! So after finally taking a few photographs where she was—side-on only was the best she could manage—she returned determinedly to a point near both Court and the branding fire.

'I notice on one of the mud maps *Alick*,' pointedly stressed, 'obtained for me this morning, that the area surrounding the homestead to—oh, about five or ten miles out, appears to be completely fenced off,' she began with cool efficiency, her gaze holding Court's tenaciously. 'Is there any particular reason for that?'

He studied her silently for an unsettling moment. 'Since the property comprises something like a thousand square miles—all of which is criss-crossed with a maze of, to the uninitiated, confusing tracks—for the most part it's a precaution against any—er—inexperienced visitors inadvertently becoming lost,' he relayed finally with a touch of mockery Eden deduced was aimed at her own lack of awareness, and her cheeks warmed discomfitingly as a result.

Nevertheless, she refused to drop her gaze, but forced herself to continue by prompting, 'For the most part. . .?'

Court bent down to extract an iron from the fire. 'It also ensures that the main cattle areas are left undisturbed.'

Eden assimilated the information contemplatively as he proceeded to brand the calf held in the crush, her next question already formulated by the time he returned the iron to the fire.

'And the wildlife safaris mentioned in your present brochure? Are they also for the same length of time as the camp-out trail rides?'

'Not usually,' Court replied briefly as, along with
another of the ringers, he went about opening and
shutting some of the various gates controlling the
race and the crush.

Suspecting him of being deliberately uninforma-
tive, Eden dogged his steps persistently. 'Well, how
long are they for, then?'

Court expelled a slow breath—as if his patience
was coming to an end. 'Since they're conducted in
four-wheel-drive vehicles, normally just a day.' He
paused, one dark brow peaking sardonically. 'And
now, if you've quite finished, perhaps you might
allow us *both* to get on with what we're supposed to
be doing without any further interruptions!' He
began moving away again.

'Oh, but. . .'

'Photograph!' The order was snapped out with the
same unyielding brevity as he had used earlier in the
morning and, like then, Eden surmised she would
merely be wasting her breath by attempting to dispute the direction—despite the aggravated feelings it
aroused within her. She had only been trying to show
an interest in her supposedly prospective work, when
all was said and done!

The one activity she hadn't photographed in the
yards so far was the calves being branded, and as it
happened this turned out to be rather more difficult
than she anticipated. For even with the top half of
the stable door-designed side of the crush opened to
facilitate the procedure, it still proved hard to get a
decent view of the animals owing to their smaller size,
and she was almost about to give the idea away altogether when the ringer who happened to be operating

the equipment at the time offered a helpful solution.

'Would you like me to open the lower door as well next time?' he enquired on noticing her frustrated efforts.

'Could you?' Eden greeted the suggestion both gratefully and eagerly. 'It would certainly make a much better picture with the whole of the calf in, rather than just its head and a little of its back.'

'Sure, I can do that for you,' the young man agreed with an easy smile, and after allowing a couple of already marked cows through to the dip, proceeded to trap the head of the following and somewhat smaller heifer between the front holding gates.

Thinking to save the ringer the necessity of moving in order to unlatch the bottom door since the catches were nearer to where she was standing, Eden did it for him and had swung the door wide before the man's urgent call to, 'Hold it!' could stop her. Surprised, she looked at him quizzically as the full side of the calf was momentarily exposed, and then swallowed in dismay when the animal suddenly scrambled backwards and, seeing the opening now presented, lauched itself through it and into the yard in a flurry of skittering feet.

The ringer promptly made a grab for it, but now that the already nervous heifer was free it obviously meant to make the most of it. Evading the man's arms, it careered past Eden at a speed that had her jumping aside hurriedly as it headed straight through the fire, scattering irons and burning logs in all directions.

Court and the other two men also immediately gave chase, while outside the yard those visitors still watching not surprisingly took advantage of the situation with their cameras. Something Eden wasn't able to do, for after her first horrified realisation at what she had unwittingly allowed to happen, her second thought had been for her camera bag beneath the tree, and it was to protect the valuable equipment within it that she raced across the yard. To her relief she discovered Alick had already seen to that on her behalf, and was even then sitting on the top rail surrounding the enclosure, her bag in hand, watching the scene below with open amusement.

'You'd better get yourself up here too, unless you've got an urge to be knocked flying,' he advised Eden with a smile.

'By the calf. . . or Court?' she hazarded in eloquent accents as she complied somewhat awkwardly with his suggestion because of the camera strung around her neck.

'The calf, of course,' he laughed.

Eden wasn't so confident, particularly in view of the considerable time and effort it required before the extremely fractious heifer was finally captured and returned to the holding yard—a scene she did succeed in photographing.

'How in hell did that happen?' demanded Court of Eden's helpful ringer on their return to the crush, but to her relief in more rueful tones than infuriated ones.

The younger man shrugged. 'The head wasn't properly secured before the lower door was opened.'

'Why in blazes would you open the lower door, anyway?' Court eyed him with a frown.

Down on the ground again now, it was Eden who answered. 'He didn't—I did,' she owned. 'But too soon, apparently.' She sent the ringer a regretful glance. 'I'm sorry.'

'That's okay.' He shook his head, smiling, to dismiss her apology.

Noting the action, Court's features took on an irritated look before his ebony framed eyes connected with Eden's. 'I guess I should have known *you* would have a hand in it somewhere,' he delared with heavy sarcasm. 'It's coming to be about par for the course!'

Eden's cheeks filled with colour, but as much as she disliked the evaluation there was, unfortunately, little she could put forward in her own defence in view of her performance to date. 'Yes—well—I'm sorry,' she offered diffidently instead. She supposed he was entitled to that much at least. 'I'll try to ensure nothing similiar happens again.'

'That would be an improvement!' There was no lessening of the mockery in his tone.

'Oh, give her a go, Court!' Alick now broke in to urge. 'It could have happened to anyone, and it's not as if it caused you *that* much trouble.'

'Although not as a result of your participation!' his stepbrother immediately retorted drily.

'What, in these?' Alick glanced down at his stylish shirt and pants. 'Not likely!' he grinned.

'Hmm. . .' An oblique twist caught at Court's attractively shaped mouth, and he paused before adding smoothly, 'I was also under the impression that I *was* giving Golden Girl here a go. . . by agreeing to employ her.'

'Well, yes, of course,' Alick allowed, if with a touch of unexpected awkwardness. 'Something Eden and I naturally both appreciate.'

The curve to Court's lips became more chafingly conspicuous. 'Just as I'll appreciate it if you'll now

do *me* the favour of taking her away from here. . .
while the men and I do still have the chance to complete our work some time before nightfall!'

Nettled by his last comment, which she considered
an unfair exaggeration, Eden consequently wasn't
prepared to be so meekly obliging, especially when it
had been his instruction that she take photographs
in the first place.

'Oh, but I haven't finished yet,' she defied, her chin
lifting fractionally higher.

'Don't take any bets on that!' Court's prompt
return was delivered in annoyingly goading accents.
He sent his stepbrother a graphic glance and gestured with his head towards the gate. 'Out!'

'You're the boss,' Alick acquiesced with a smile in
his customary easygoing fashion, and with little
choice now but to do the same, Eden grudgingly
accompanied him from the yards.

'Well, it appears I did manage to have myself banished, after all,' she remarked with partly disgruntled,
partly rueful flippancy as they headed back to the
complex.

'Although not before you obtained some of the
information you wanted,' Alick was quick to remind
him.

There was that, she supposed with a sigh. Not that
it seemed much consolation at the moment.

'So where to now?' he went on to enquire casually,
apparently considering the other matter satisfactor-
ily concluded.

Shrugging off the slight feeling of despondency
that had started to assail her, Eden deliberated for a
second or two before proposing, 'If possible, it had
better be the river, I guess.' Adding in a lighter vein

as she attempted to match his unconcerned mood, 'I should be able to get all the rest of the necessary photos around here at any time, but after this morning's efforts, there's no telling how long it might be before I'm permitted to go further afield.'

His lips twitched at the ironic inflection in her voice. You've got your own set of wheels,' he pointed out humorously. 'So there's nothing to stop you from doing a little exploring if you feel like it. Provided you're careful, you should be able to manage most of the tracks within the fenced portion of the property without a four-wheel-drive, except for a couple of the creek and river crossings, of course.'

Eden pursed her lips contemplatively, and nodded. She hadn't thought of that.

'However, if it's still the river you want, then the river it will be,' he continued. 'We can collect a packed lunch from the kitchen, pick up a four-wheel-drive from the garage, and be on our way almost immediately. That suit you?'

'Sounds fine,' she confirmed, and half an hour or so later was taking her seat next to him inside one of the station's Land Rovers.

'Oh, yes, I can't remember whether it's mentioned in the present brochure or not, but there's also a couple of these available for hire,' Alick advised, motioning with a hand to the vehicle. 'The majority of those who arrive by road come by four-wheel-drive, of course, but those who fly in don't have that advantage, so these are to enable them to get around the property as well. And as you can see, this is the collection and returning point for the boats.' The addition was made as they left the buildings behind and began travelling alongside a wide, tree-lined

creek where a couple of the said craft could be seen
tied up at a small landing. 'If I remember correctly,
Simone used to have a book where she noted any
reservations and so on concerning both the vehicles
and the boats, so that's probably something you
could take over immediately. I expect you'll find the
book somewhere in the office.'

'Won't someone complain, though,'—she meant
Court specifically—'if I just go rummaging through
there looking for it?'

'I don't see why they should. You're on the staff,
after all.'

Although only in a manner of speaking, it seemed
to her.

For the remainder of the time available before he
had to leave, they continued in much the same way:
Alick relaying whatever information he could about
the area, including the recommended fishing spots,
and Eden mentally storing each fact away as best she
could, the whole interspersed with periodic halts for
the taking of more photographs.

It was all completely new to her, and she was anxious to learn as much as possible from him in as short
a time as possible. When all was said and done, when
he left on the mail plane that afternoon, she would
virtually be on her own. A circumstance she wasn't
particularly looking forward to, and nervously disclosed as much while waiting on the airstrip with him
later in the day as Gaye Redman exchanged the
property's outgoing mail bag for the incoming one
with the pilot.

'As I told you yesterday, you worry too much,'
Alick tried to overcome her misgivings with an
encouraging smile. 'After all, the hardest part—per-

suading Court to accept the idea—is over. All you have to do now is settle in and prove me right.'

Eden wasn't so sure—of either statement! 'That could be extremely difficult to achieve if he continues to refuse to give me any relevant directions like he did today,' she disputed in mocking despair.

'Then don't let him! Hassle him into telling you what you want to know—follow him to wherever he's gone even, if you have to—but don't take no for an answer!'

'Hassle him!' she repeated incredulously. 'That's all right for you to say, you're part of the family. Judging by this morning's reaction, it would probably just get me fired!'

'For making enquiries about your work?' he countered expressively, brows lifting. 'That would certainly be unique. Besides, running the tourist side of things is what he's supposedly paying you for, and reluctant or not, he's still not the type to happily keep paying for something he's not receiving.'

'Which brings us to my exit once again!'

Alick shook his head in veto. 'Which brings us to Court finally leaving all such arrangements to you. . . because you've proved by what you *have* taken over—the boat and vehicle hire, for instance— that you can manage them.'

He made it sound a foregone conclusion, and yet. . . And yet Eden wasn't even certain just why she was willing to subject herself to all the vexation in the first place! It would have been all so much less bother just to return to Townsville. Perhaps it was simply a case of refusing to accept defeat before she had even had a chance to prove herself, she decided.

'Sorry to interrupt, Alick, but it's time we were leaving.' The pilot's voice fragmented Eden's thoughts as he spoke to the man beside her after having stowed his bag and the mail in the small plane.

'Yeah, sure, Laurie, I'll be right with you,' Alick turned to reply. To Eden he half smiled apologetically, 'I've got to go, sweetie, but you just do as I've said and everything will be fine, okay?'

Exhaling heavily, resignedly, her expression turned wry. 'Is that a promise?'

He grinned and bent down to kiss her lightly on the forehead. 'Just about,' he declared confidently. 'So stop looking as if the world's about to come to an end, hmm? I'm only a phone call away should you ever feel in need of any advice, in any case.'

'That could be daily,' she quipped, not entirely mirthfully.

'You'll manage,' he insisted, smiling, as he turned to board the plane.

Eden only wished she could view the matter with equal assurance, but despite her apprehensions still managed to give him a smile and a wave in return before he entered the aircraft.

In no time at all, the plane was back in the air once more, heading for other properties and isolated towns along its route to home base, and with a last wave as it banked over head Eden turned to head back to the homestead—and discovered Gaye Redman standing a couple of yards behind her.

CHAPTER FOUR

'IT SEEMED a good opportunity to meet you since I understand you're going to be working here too, so I thought I'd wait,' the girl explained with a friendly smile. 'You're Eden, aren't you?'

Eden nodded, smiling herself, and grateful for the genial overture. 'While you're Gaye.'

'I can see Alick's been talking!' that girl laughed. She paused slightly. 'I suppose you're disappointed to see him leave again so soon too.'

Despite experiencing a little surprise at the assumption, Eden merely shrugged deprecatingly. 'Only in so far as he was the only one I could really talk to, as I don't yet know anyone else here.' She cast the other girl an interested glance as, by common though unspoken assent, they began walking back toward the complex. 'Have you worked here long yourself?'

'Almost two years now.'

'And you like it?' probed Eden, speculating that if Gaye did, then there should be no reasons for her not to either, at least in time.

'Oh, yes!' Gaye's answer was emphatic, and reassuring. Before continuing, she climbed between the rails of the white-painted fence that surrounded the complex instead of walking down to the gate, and waited while Eden did the same. 'The staff here are all very nice too. Well, maybe except for Crystal when she gets all haughty and officious,' she inserted with a rueful laugh as they skirted a pair of long-legged red and grey brolgas that were stepping regally across the closely mown grass. 'While as for the boss. . . well, as I expect you've already discovered for yourself, he's really a honey, and I think just about every girl on the staff is, secretly at least, a little crazy about him.'

'Yes, well, he's certainly good-looking,' Eden allowed grudgingly against her present inclinations to find anything praiseworthy about Court, but knowing her companion was doubtless expecting some comment of the kind.

Not that it stopped her from changing the subject to more general topics immediately thereafter, however, which kept them occupied until they reached the office, where Gaye deposited the dark blue mail bag on a chair and, as her presence was required in the bar, had to depart.

Left on her own, Eden hovered uncertainly just inside the doorway, deliberating whether to search for the book noting the reservations of the boats and vehicles as Alick had said she should, or not. Eventually, it ws the thought that if she didn't she would quite possibly be relinquishing any chance of forcing Court into finally accepting her as Tourist Manager that decided her and, squaring her shoulders, she made for the desk determinedly to set about sorting through the mounds of papers, ledgers, and other notebooks littering the top of the heavy timber writing table.

As it happened, her decision paid dividends, for soon her search not only uncovered the book she had been seeking, but a host of other relevant material also, including an accommodation register for the lodge units, an accounts book for the campers' fees, plus a sheet detailing all the tours, trail rides, plane flights and so on, that could be arranged as well.

Delighted though she was with her discoveries, before she began to thoroughly acquaint herself with them Eden still proceeded to look about the room for anything else than might also prove relevant, her eyes finally alighting on a label-making gadget on the shelves that lined part of one wall, plus a couple of cartons of T-shirts—presumably replacement stock for the small souvenir counter she had seen the previous afternoon tucked away in one corner of the bar area. And in actual fact, it was to those two latter items that she directed her attention first. The label-maker, to enable her to print out her name and position, and with the aid of a thin piece of white cardboard and a large pin fashion herself a badge to wear that would immediately inform people who she was and why she was there, because she strongly suspected that if *she* didn't advertise the fact, it wouldn't be circulated at all! The T-shirts she merely deemed appropriate gear for her to wear, and after searching through the cartons and selecting a sleeveless, scooped-neck design, bearing on one side of the neckline, a small reproduction of the property's logo—the head of an Australian-bred Droughtmaster bull, with the name of the station above it and a scroll detailing the branding mark below—she picked out four in a variety of colours. Then she concentrated on learning what she could from the books she had uncovered.

It proved to be an exercise that took longer than Eden expected, so that by the time she had finished the sounds coming from the bar next door were considerably louder as more and more people dropped in to have a drink and share their day's experiences. Leaving all the books, except the one used for the reservations of the boats and vehicles—in view of Court apparently not utilising it, she felt entitled to retain that one, but as yet just wasn't confident enought, personally or in her position, to take the chance on doing the same with the others—she decided to return to the homestead and made her way towards the back door of the building.

'Oh, there you are!' Crystal's disdainful voice sounded behind her as the girl entered the passageway from the bar and made for the door leading into the kitchen. 'There's a call coming through on the radio in the bar—someone wanting to make a booking, I expect. Gaye mentioned you were in the office, so in view of you being our new Tourist Manager, I was sure you wouldn't want anyone else dealing with it. You can take it on Channel 2.'

'But I don't know how to use a transceiver!' Eden exclaimed, aghast, swinging back to face her—and just as she surmised Crystal would also be very much aware.

'Oh, but for someone as—er—enterprising as you, I've no doubt you'll be able to overcome that small setback with the same ease with which you managed to manoeuvre yourself in here,' Crystal proposed disparagingly before disappearing into the kitchen.

Left holding the bag, as it were, Eden supposed she had little choice but to do what she could, and only hoped that perhaps Gaye would be in the bar to render some assistance. It was obvious Crystal wasn't going to! Hurrying back into the office, she collected a pen and the relevant book she had been perusing such a short time before, then caught her breath in hope on suddenly realising that the now fading whirring sound coming from outside meant that the helicopters had returned. There was just the chance that Court might have been waiting for them and, consequently, accompany the pilots into the bar, she prayed, because on this occasion she was more than willing to have him deal with the matter. The more so when, on entering the area, she discovered Gaye to be nowhere in sight.

However, instead of having to cross apprehensively to the radio which occupied a shelf behind the small souvenir counter, she now threaded her way hastily between the various groups of people to wait anxiously at the top of the steps leading on to the veranda in order to ensure she was the first to speak to Court, if he did indeed arrive.

A few minutes later, Eden heaved a heartfelt sigh of relief at having her hunch proved correct on seeing him approach, along with Joel and the four pilots. Her amber gaze fastened to him as he moved closer, her pulse abruptly leaping involuntarily as he responded with a laugh to something Joel said. Dark and vital, his movements filled with an unconscious strength and assurance, there was a strongly male aura about him, a magnetic presence, that she suddenly found extremely disturbing and in consequence had her dragging her eyes away to concentrate on Joel's less disconcerting features instead.

Nick, one of the two pilots she had met the evening before and who had been most attentive during dinner, was the first to begin mounting the steps. 'Dare I hope it's me you're waiting to welcome home after a hard day's mustering?' he grinned banteringly up at her.

'Sorry,' she apologised with a smiling shake of her head. 'Actually, it's Court I wanted to have a word with.' She reluctantly returned a somewhat self-conscious gaze in the latter's direction, and saw his brows peak with a wry expressiveness.

'I guess I should have known it was too much to expect,' lamented Nick in extravagant tones of mock despair.

'Mmm, she does appear to have too much sense to want to associate with you, doesn't she?' quipped Larry, the other pilot she had met the previous night, as he followed him on to the veranda.

'Thanks! A great mate you turned out to be!' retorted Nick as the pair of them continued on towards the bar. Although he obviously couldn't resist adding over his shoulder, 'Don't pay any attention to him, Eden! He's just put out because he knows he lacks my gifts and flair when it comes to the opposite sex.'

It was a chaffing piece of raillery that, not unexpectedly, brought hoots of derisive laughter, and a number of similarly taunting comments from his companions as they also headed into the bar, but which Eden only acknowledged rather absently as her attention remained on her employer.

'So what's so urgent, or important, that you felt it necessary to inform me the moment I returned, hmm?' Court drawled lazily, coming to a halt beside her. 'You created more mayhem somewhere else now?'

'No!' she denied infuriatedly, her colour rising uncontrollably at the mocking reminder. 'I merely wanted to advise you as soon as possible that there's call coming though on the radio, apparently, and since I don't know how to operate a transceiver, I just thought it best for you to take it.'

'In that case. . .' He dropped a hand on to her shoulder to begin propelling her along with him into the bar. 'So why didn't Crystal take it?' A lazy-lidded but alert aquamarine gaze was slanted downwards.

Eden shrugged evasively as they wound their way to the back of the bar, not wanting to be the cause of any repercussions perhaps eventuating as a result of any disclosure she might make. 'She wasn't available at the time,' she temporised.

'Then who took the message in the first place?'

'I wouldn't know.' Well, she certainly couldn't be sure it had been Crystal. But as they had now reached the radio, she went on swiftly in the hope of forestalling any further questions, 'I've brought the reservations book and a pen with me.'

'Have you now?' Court eyed her ironically, and a new wave of colour stained her cheeks as she realised she had inadvertently revealed that, just by have the book, she must have made use of the office during his absence. 'And what makes you think they'll be necessary?'

'Because. . .' Eden only just managed to swallow the name that had been about to trip off the end of her tongue, but still couldn't quite continue to hold his discomfiting gaze. Instead, she made a play of opening the book to its correct page while offering with false brightness, 'Because it's always a possibility, isn't it?' Then she turned her attention to the static-marred conversation that was already emanating from the receiver.

Briefly, she could sense Court continuing to watch her, but refused to look up, and then she heard a faint exhalation of breath as he turned one of the knobs on the radio, picked up the hand-piece and began transmitting.

'7QZY calling VJI. . . I understand you've a telephone call for us, Gavin.'

Despite not always being able to catch everything that was being said at the other end because of static, Eden watched and listened with great interest when the call was subsequently put through—on Channel 2, and proving to be someone wanting to make a booking, all as Crystal had suggested. She considered it quite possible that the other girl might attempt the same again, and apart from finding it enlightening in any case, she wanted to be prepared.

'So you didn't know who took the message, and Crystal wasn't available, huh?' A sardonic slope edge one corner of Court's mouth upwards as he turned to face her when he had finished.

Eden's amber eyes widened slightly. How had he apparently found that out? 'I don't know what you mean,' she stalled.

'Oh, don't give me that, honey!' he retorted on a shortening note. 'You heard, the same as I did, when Gavin said he was surprised that Crystal hadn't taken the call herself!'

So that was what had surprised him! 'Except that I—I couldn't make out all he said because of the crackling,' she explained hesitantly.

'You didn't need to! You evidently already knew!' He drew a deep breath, his darkly lashed eyes holding hers unwaveringly. 'And now maybe you'd care to disclose just why Crystal didn't take the call!

Because it was something else you considered you should be doing, only when you discovered it was a little more difficult than you imagined, you decided to pass it on to me?'

'No!' she gasped, partly in dismay, partly in annoyance that he should have chosen to have put such a construction on her actions. 'Although I suppose I should really have expected you to come to a conclusion like that! After all, just because I was waiting for you when you returned, you immediately had to think I'd bungled something!' She glared at him huffily.

'Something *else!*' Court still had no compunction in amending, sarcastically. 'And if it's such a erroneous conclusion, then don't damn well lie to me, honey, by pretending ignorance when I ask you a question! I've neither the time nor the patience for it! So *was* it Crystal who decided to play cute by passing the call on to you—as I originally suspected—or wasn't it?'

Eden shifted uncomfortably from one foot to the other before finally giving a reluctant nod.

'Well, *thank you* for the truth at last!' he mocked sardonically. 'You certainly like to make a person work for it, don't you?'

'Only because I didn't want to be the cause of any trouble!' she defended in flaring accents, feeling both wronged and irritated. 'Particularly as you were available to take the call, anyway!'

'Which is neither here nor there! So in future, how about you just stick to the facts, and let *me* decide if any trouble is going to ensue or not, hmm?'

Eden hunched one shoulder in a manner that could have been acquiescent, or defiant, and cast a covert look about the room from beneath long, curling lashes, half expecting to discover everyone looking in their direction. On gratefully noting that, in actual fact, no one seemed to be paying them any undue attention whatsoever, he inclined her head higher.

'Then if that's all. . .' She gathered up the pen and book again, as well as the T-shirts she had automatically brought with her when she left the office, preparing to leave.

'Not quite,' Court drawled, and barred her exit by the simple expedient of bringing one hand to rest on the counter. 'Now that we're on the subject, maybe it's appropriate I find out just what else you've been doing since this morning. That is, apart from apparently having gone through the office with a fine-tooth comb, of course.' His mouth sloped expressively as he eyed the bundle in her arms.

'Except that I didn't go through it with a fine-tooth comb!' she immediately denied hotly. 'I merely checked through those items that were on the desk in order to familiarise myself with matters relating to my position here! That is, *if* I'm ever to be allowed to fulfil it properly!' Sarcasm laced her voice.

'As to that, I guess you'll just have to wait until, once again, *I* decide whether you're capable of doing so, won't you?'

Implying that, that was the reason he was so reluctant to actually give her any responsibility? Also doubtless enforced by her stupidity of that morning, she supposed. 'A decision that could be an extremely long time coming if I'm never to have the opportunity to prove my ability!' she still gibed, undeterred.

Court flexed a denim-clad shoulder with negligent grace. 'I'm giving you the chance to photograph the place for the new brochure. Even suggested myself that's what you should do today, if it comes to that,' he put forward, but in such a chaffing fashion that she could have hit him.

And that was in spite of the fact that in other circumstances, she was well aware she would have been more than happy just to be given such an opportunity. 'Although, in this case, simply in order to prevent me from doing anything else!' she fumed.

He slanted an explicit gaze towards the bundle in her arms once more. 'But not very successfully, it would appear.'

'Well, not even you could expect someone to take photos all day, every day!'

'Nevertheless. . .' He caught her off guard by unexpectedly running a finger along the line of her jaw in a leisurely warning that, to her consternation, left her feeling waywardly tantalised rather than threatened. 'I hope you didn't see fit to ignore my instructions altogether.'

'Would I dare?' she quipped with edgy pertness due top her still flustered state.

'In the interests of. . .'

'Oh, don't worry, I can assure you I did as ordered first,' she cut in with something of a snap, recovering at last, and furious with herself for having permitted a mere touch to have had such an effect on her. 'I spent most of the afternoon photographing too, you'll be pleased to hear.'

'Within the complex?' A light taunting half-smile began playing about the edges of his shapely mouth.

'As a matter of fact, no, not exactly,' Eden divulged, returning his gaze somewhat challengingly. He *had* made a point of wanting to hear the truth, when all was said and done, and what would have been the point in prevaricating when it would have been only too easy for him to discover that she had been away from the homestead area for the best part of the day? 'Before he left, Alick was kind enough to show me both the south and north arms of the river, as well as some of the immediate countryside.' She paused, tilting her head slightly to one side and casting him a deliberately piquant glance from between her lashes as she recalled Alick's comment on the subject. 'Besides, you did only *suggest* that I remain around the homestead, didn't you?'

Court's half-smile widened to show even white teeth, and had Eden's heart skipping a beat. This was a side of her employer that she hadn't witnessed before, and she was starting to appreciate how all the girls on the property's staff could, apparently, have flipped a little over him. 'An oversight on my part, evidently,' he drawled in whimsical tones.

'But not one you're going to correct?' she hazarded quickly, her expression turning anxious.

His lips quirked with ironic humour. 'I sense it wouldn't have much effect even if I did.'

Eden's face cleared magically as she tried hard to repress a smile. 'Well, you couldn't really expect. . .'

'Don't labour the point, honey, or I may have second thoughts,' he inserted wryly with a cautioning shake of his head. 'Try explaining what you're doing with all those instead.' He gestured to the package T-shirts.

'These?' She looked downwards in surprise at the sudden change in subject. A dismaying thought sprang to mind, and she immediately sought to assure him, 'Oh, I intent to pay for them. I wasn't just helping myself, if that's what you're thinking.'

'It wasn't,' drily. 'I was merely curious as to why you would want so many.'

'Oh!' she said again, but on a relieved note this time. 'Well, I just thought they would be appropriate for me to wear in my—er—*supposed* position as Tourist Manager,' she relayed with an uncontrollable pointed emphasis. 'They're a good promotion for the property, and. . .' she hesitated a little, then rushed on almost defiantly, '... and I hoped it might help the visitors to recognise me.'

'I see,' Court mused lazily, his darkly outlined eyes surveying her measuringly. 'You reckon they'll need help to recognise someone who stands out a mile from among the rest anyway?'

Unsure whether his words had been meant as a compliment—which seemed unlikely—or as a reproval—which she considered for more probable—Eden elected not to answer directly. 'I meant, in my role as—as Tourist Manager.' The fact that she had also manufactured a badge declaring herself as such, she judiciously decided not to reveal.

'To which end you were also planning on confiscating that, I presume?' Nodding to the smaller book she held.

Trust him to have noticed it! She ran the tip of her tongue nervously across her lips. It was hard to gauge from his demeanour precisely how he felt about her action in this regard and, as a result, her response was guardedly and awkwardly made.

'Yes—well—in view of the last entry having been made some months ago, I—I thought I could perhaps make—er—use of it instead.'

'In what way?'

As if he didn't already know! 'In—in noting who wanted the boats or vehicles, for how long, and—and when.'

Court shrugged. 'That would simply make for confusion and mistakes, wouldn't it? Not to mention being superfluous, since I already have all that information in here.' He trapped a finger against his temple.

'Not if there was only one of us doing it!' Eden persisted doggedly.

'There is.'

The implication was plain, even if she was loath to accept it. 'But why not me? It can hardly be a complicated task, and surely you're going to have to let me do *something* some time!'

'I was under the impression I already had. The photos. . . remember?' He arched a well-defined brow goadingly.

Oh, yes, she supposed he *was* in the position where he could find something amusing in the situation! Eden smouldered. 'All of which you no doubt intend to dismiss out of hand, anyhow!' she charged acidly.

'Quite possibly. . . if I consider them neither suitable nor good enough,' Court wasn't averse to owning. 'Although we'll never know until you finish them, will we? So why don't you just concentrate on the work you've been allocated, and leave me to attend to the rest, huh?'

Eden's eyes sparkled mutinously. 'Meaning, you don't believe I'm capable of undertaking a whole *two* tasks simultaneously, is that it?' she demanded, sarcasm predominant.

'Meaning, don't push your luck too hard, Golden Girl,' his warning surfaced as a mocking drawl. 'Be satisfied with the win you've already had, or you might yet find your freedom restricted. Do I make myself clear?'

'Abundantly!' she snapped. And this was the man Alick had told her to hassle! He had to have been joking. . . or thinking of someone else!

'Right! That's good,' Court approved with a lazily knowing smile that had Eden railing at herself furiously for being unable to control the effect it had on her after all he'd just had to say. 'Now you'd better come and meet Neil and Hew, the other two chopper drivers. I don't expect you've met many of the other people here yet.' He caught hold of her wrist in a light grip and began moving out from behind the counter.

Surprised that he should be willing to take it on himself to introduce her to the two men, and despite a certain wistfulness at feeling such an outsider, Eden still broke free again almost immediately.

'I think I'll give it a miss, if you don't mind! I'm really not in the mood for socialising at the moment, and I'm sure you would prefer to see these,' nodding towards the books, 'out of my possession and back in the office as soon as possible, in any case,' she declared in satirical accents.

'If I did, I would have said so, believe me!' he retorted. 'So stop sulking just because you failed to get your own way for once, and come and have a drink. You can leave these here.' He calmly relieved her of everything she was carrying and deposited it all on the shelf beside the radio.

Eden didn't protest because she was already gasping with indignation. 'What do you mean, failed to get my own way *for once*? I'm not accustomed to always getting my own way! Nor am I sulking either!'

'Good! Then there's no reason for you not to come and meet the others, is there?' he immediately countered, tauntingly. 'While as for not being used to getting your own way. . .' His lips curved crookedly. 'You surprise me. The way you seem to have already got all the men here that you have met so ready to support you, I wouldn't have thought there had been any who'd denied you much.'

'With you providing the exception, of course!' she was quick to snipe.

'Which is something to be grateful for at least, I guess,' his return quip was expressively voiced, and seemingly considered the matter as settled, he took hold of her wrist again and began leading her across the room to the table where the others were seated.

This time Eden acquiesced, not only because she was interested in meeting more of the people who worked on the property, but also to avoid being accused once more of sulking—or worse!—if she refused.

Neil and Hew proved to be another two likeable young men in their early twenties, the same as Nick and Larry, and only too willing to answer any of Eden's questions regarding the work they undertook. That it could also be a very risky business on occasion, she soon came to realise, although from their attitudes and remarks she strongly suspected it was precisely that element of danger that attracted all four of them. As Larry had happily imparted at one junctre, 'It can sure give the old adrenalin a buzz!'

'And there's enough work here for you all to be employed by the station permanently?' Eden asked

Nick, who had managed to ensure ensure that she was seated next to him.

'Oh, we're not part of the staff on Arrunga River. We're just working here under contract at the moment,' he explained. 'We're actually employed by Gulf Aerial Musters, who send us to whichever properties require our services. Like, in a couple of days we'll be heading down to Summerhill Station for a day or so, then we'll return here for another week before putting in a few days over on Iandra, and so on until everyone's mustering is completed.'

Eden nodded. 'Then what?'

'Then the rains come, which prevents just about all movement, of stock and everything else, and we head south for a three-month holiday,' he grinned.

'Half your luck!' she laughed eloquently.

'Mmm, it's a pretty good life, and you certainly get to see a good deal of the country up here, as well as meet a lot of friendly people. And talking of people—I'm meeting a couple of friends for dinner at the pub in Torrington this evening. The meals may not be quite up to the standard here, but it still makes something of a change.' Pausing, he eyed her in hopeful enquiry. 'I don't suppose you'd care to join us? You'd be most welcome, if you did, and I'm sure you'd like them. Ray's old man owns the hotel, and Sally's a real livewire.'

Caught unprepared by the invitation, Eden wasn't quite sure how to answer for a moment. 'I—well. . .' she faltered, her gaze, for some unknown reason, involuntarily swinging in Court's direction as if seeking his reaction, but only to find his attention now engaged by a visitor who had stopped by his chair to question him about something. Then, annoyed with herself for having done anything of the kind—heavens above, she surely didn't need his permission to go out with anyone!—she looked back at Nick, her decision made. 'Thank you, I'd love to come. Although it's a long and somewhat strenuous drive,' drily, 'to suffer just for dinner, isn't it?' She remembered Torrington—one hotel, a post office, a general store-cum service station, the old council chambers, and little else—from when she and Alick had passed through it the day before. She also remembered the dust-covered, pot-holed, vehicle-destroying road they'd had to travel on from there to the Arrunga River turnoff!

'Drive?' Nick started to laugh. 'Sweetheart, when you've got a chopper sitting out there,' gesturing towards the airstrip, 'believe me, you don't *drive* anywhere!'

'No, I suppose not,' she allowed, smiling at her own lack of insight. 'So what time will we need to leave, then?'

Nick glanced at his watch. 'Oh, in about half an hour or so, I guess. But here,' nodding to indicate the bar, 'about now, I should say, if I'm to get cleaned up in time.' He eyed his work-stained clothes ruefully.

'In that case, I'd better be making a move to shower and change too,' Eden proposed, beginning to push back her chair.

'I'll leave with you,' he nodded, and draining the last of the beer in his can, gained his feet to pull her seat the rest of the way out for her. 'Well, we're off to hit the high spots of Torrington.' His advice to the others at the table was delivered with a grin. 'Don't wait up for us.'

Not unexpectedly, his words brought forth a number of pertinent, bantering responses, although not from Court, Eden noted. In fact, he appeared to find nothing amusing, or pleasing, in the situation at all, and she experienced a feeling of slight surprise on connecting with his narrowed, dissecting gaze. Then she gave a shrug and wondered why she should have found his reaction the least unusual. After all, nothing else she had done so far seemed to have pleased him either!

CHAPTER FIVE

AFTER a late but very enjoyable night, Eden didn't wake until almost eight the next morning, but on recalling that she was only supposed to be taking more photos that day, and the light for such photography wouldn't be at its best for another couple of hours, she continued to lie in bed for a while, musing over the events of the previous evening.

Their meal had been plain and plentiful rather than elaborate, and the company extremely pleasant and relaxing—something she had very much appreciated after her somewhat less than auspicious first day on the station. The flights to and from town—her first in a helicopter—and despite its being too dark to actually see much, she had also found very pleasurable, particularly when compared to the lengthier and certainly far less comfortable trip by road. As an escort Nick had proved to be attentive, amusing and informative, and if his goodnight kiss hadn't precisely set any bells ringing, then at the same time it hadn't been unpleasant either, and she wasn't really looking to become involved in any heavy relationships anyway.

Footsteps in the hallway outside her room were what eventually interrupted Eden's reverie and had her stirring from her bed as she speculated who it might be. Court and Joel would be long gone, she was sure. After pulling on her wrapper and opening her door, however, she was surprised to discover that it was indeed Joel, after all.

'Sorry, did I wake you?' He was the first to speak. Then, with a grin, 'I gather you can't have returned until quite late last night.' He continued almost immediately, 'But now I'm afraid I'd better collect what I came for and be on my way.'

'How come you're so much later in leaving than yesterday, though?' Eden enquired interestedly before he could move off. 'Aren't you taking part in the muster today?' She knew from what Nick had told her that there was one scheduled, and spared a sympathetic thought for him at having to be on the job again so early after their late night.

He nodded. 'Uh-huh! Although on the ground with the ringers today. Bryan and I are just about to leave with the truck.'

Eden suddenly had an idea. 'Would I be able to go with you?' she asked eagerly.

Joel's expression turned apologetic. 'Well, if you'd been ready, you probably could have, but as it is I'm afraid Bryan will start doing his block if I don't get down to the garage shortly. We're already late in leaving now. Perhaps some other time, hmm?'

'I suppose it will have to be,' she sighed with evident disappointment.

'Or, if you've got one of those maps of the place, I could show you the general area where we're likely to be and you could follow the truck's tyre tracks out there,' he proposed abruptly, obviously attempting to be as helpful as he could.

'Oh, that would be great!' Eden enthused, her demeanour brightening again immediately. 'I've got one right here.' She raced back into her room to collect the map Alick had given her the day before.

Of necessity, as the station's overseer was waiting, Joel's instructions were brief and roughly marked on the sheet of paper, but they still sounded straight-forward enough, and Eden was certain she would have no difficulty in locating the mustering team.

'Anyway, as I first mentioned, you should be able to follow our tracks easily enough even without hav-ing to resort to the map,' Joel concluded reassuringly.

'I'm sure I will, and thank you,' she smiled grate-fully. 'Oh. . .' a slight frown had her winged brows suddenly drawing closer together, 'will I be able to make it in my own car, though?'

He shook his head. 'No, you'd better take one of the four-wheel-drives. I doubt you'd make it across Stockyard Creek in a car, or if you did, you'd have water all through the inside of it. Just see Jim—Jim Stanley—down at the machine sheds before you leave, and he'll check that you've sufficient fuel, and all, okay?'

She nodded quickly, but purposely refrained from asking whether she would actually be required to utilise its four-wheel-drive capabilities, because she hadn't ever driven such a vehicle before. That was something else she could check with Jim Stanley, she decided.

And within a very short time, after washing and dressing in jeans, sneakers, and a sleeveless check shirt, loading her camera gear into the vehicle, and gulping down a cup of hot tea and some toast, that was exactly what she was doing. Seeking and receiv-ing some instruction from the station's lean, gruff, and grizzle-haired mechanic.

Then, primed with the necessary information which had been surprisingly kindly imparted by

someone who she had gathered from remarks made
on her first night at the station normally had little
time for women, she set off along the same track she
and Alick had followed the day before. The double
set of treadmarks from the truck's tyres were clearly
visible in the sandy soil ahead of her, and so for the
first part of her journey she was fortunately able to
concentrate most of her attention on learning to
handle the unfamiliar vehicle.

Her uneventful crossing of Saltwater Creek—the
north arm of the Arrunga River—even though there
was only a foot or so of water in it at that point, gave
her confidence a boost for the deeper and wider south
arm that was to come.

Once she was across the creek, however, the route
the truck followed now diverged from the one she and
Alick had taken, heading further inland and into
more open terrain, a denser line of trees a couple of
miles ahead denoting the whereabouts of the south
arm of the river. Even so, the track didn't immediately lead to the crossing, Eden discovered, but
continued parallel with the tropical shrub and tree-
lined waterway for a time before the banks shelved
sufficiently for a vehicle to negotiate them, whereupon it swung downwards to the water's edge.

Momentarily, Eden brought the Land Rover to a
halt, gazing somewhat dubiously at the width and
obvious depth of the creek, and attempting to select
the exact path she should take through it in order to
avoid those dips and holes in the mainly sandy bottom which were visible through the fortunately
crystal-clear water. With a nervously drawn breath,
and the consoling thought that if others could manage it without any trouble then there really shouldn't

be any reason why she couldn't also, she faithfully followed Jim Stanley's directions and resolutely started forward again.

There was also another instruction she had been given that she kept in the forefront of her mind—that of, 'once you're into it, whatever you do, don't stop!'—and as it happened it was this piece of information more than any other, she suspected, that enabled her to actually make the crossing successfully in the end. Because at one stage, when it became apparent she couldn't evade all the hollows in the creek bed and her right front wheel seemed to sink alarmingly, it was only that thought that kept her going when otherwise she was certain she would have panicked to a halt.

With that particular obstacle now behind her, though, Eden was able to relax once more and resumed following the truck's marks in considerably higher spirits, until she presently came to the boundary fence she had questioned Court about. The steel gate across the track bore a sign declaring that staff only were permitted beyond that point—which of course she was, even if Court Buchanan was reluctant to allow her to properly fulfil her position, Eden justified.

Once through it, she began to understand just what he had meant by the area being criss-crossed with different routes, because now a surprising number of them made their appearance, veering off in all directions, and making her extremely grateful for having the truck's wheel treads to guide her. At least, that was until she emerged on to the flat, far-reaching, treeless and sparingly grassed claypans Joel had marked on her map, where after a time even the truck's tyres made no greater imprint on that hard-baked surface than all the others that had been made by a variety of previous vehicles, with the result that she eventually lost sight of them altogether.

Not unduly worried initially by their disappearance, Eden continued to drive, using Joel's rough map as a guide, in the hope of rediscovering them. When this proved fruitless, she pulled to a stop and alighted from the vehicle, hoping she might be able to pick up the sound of the helicopters and thus give herself a guide since, from the markings on the map, she presumed they should be somewhere in the not too distant vicinity.

The utter silence that greeted her, and continued unbroken by so much as the call of a bird or a rustle of the brown, bone-dry grass that grew in scattered tussocks, wasn't particularly encouraging, and at length she was forced to the disappointing conclusion that, without any definite idea as to in just which direction she should continue—it had all begun to look the same—she really had no choice but to return to the homestead. She would be foolish to take the chance on becoming hopelessly lost by continuing in the circumstances.

It wasn't until she was back in the Land Rover once more and had turned to retrace her route that she suddenly came to the dismaying realisation that she couldn't distinguish her own tracks from any of the others there either, and without any landmarks to help pinpoint just where she had emerged on to the barren claypans, her last prudent consideration had come a little too late. She had already managed to get herself lost!

Eden's initial feeling of dismay was promptly submerged beneath a censuring fury that she could have been so unbelievably incautious as to have travelled so far into the area, and changed direction so often, without once thinking to ensure she could find her way back again! *And* thereby provide Court with yet another reason to believe that she was not only irresponsible, but that she was about as intelligent as a five-year-old as well!

She had no worries that she wouldn't be found—after all, both Joel and Jim knew where she had been heading—so doubtless that would only be a matter of time. . . albeit boring, unproductive time. No, it was only her own incredible stupidity that gave her cause for despair, and trepidation at the thought of Court's likely reaction!

There was some small compensation, though, in the fact that, as it turned out, the afternoon wasn't altogether as boring and unproductive as Eden had anticipated, for at least there was the unexpected opportunity to take some photographs. First, of a mob of brumbies that came galloping on to the claypan to graze for a time, and then later of a group of wallabies as they bounded effortlessly from one side to the other. The latter, probably because of their obvious sense of direction, generated within Eden a desire to make one last determined effort to see if she couldn't discover for herself the track that led back to Stockyard Creek. But even driving to the nearest of the encircling trees and following them for what seemed mile upon mile produced no satisfactory result—she wasn't certain she was travelling in the right direction, in any case, nor that she was even in the right section of the almost circular area, if it came to that—and she was consequently forced to a halt once more to await her rescue.

When it did finally come about, it was late in the day, the sun beginning to lose its power, much to Eden's relief because she was hot, hungry, and thirsty, having had nothing to eat or drink since breakfast, although the sight of another vehicle in that desolate place had her temporarily forgetting all about any such discomforts. The fact that the ute also appeared from the direction she least expected, and some considerable distance away, but still made straight towards her as if knowing she was there, did have her brows peaking a little in surprise nonetheless.

Or, at least, that was until she realised it was Court alighting from the vehicle once it drew to a stop beside the Land Rover, whereupon she promptly began chewing her lip instead, her spirits sinking. Having recognised Bryan behind the wheel, she had hoped momentarily to perhaps be able to keep her latest blunder a secret, after all.

'And if it's not too much trouble, would you mind telling me just what the devil you're up to?' Court enquired in sardonically exasperated tones as he bent to rest tanned and sinewed forearms on the open window of the Land Rover.

Eden swallowed and lifted her head defensively. 'I—well, you can't have a brochure for a cattle station without any photos of free-ranging cattle, so I— I came to take some.'

'Here?' He swept an explicit glance over the deserted claypans.

'N-no, at the muster, actually.'

A dark brow slanted high above mocking blue-green eyes. 'It's a bit late in the day for that, isn't it? We're just about ready to leave.' He paused. '*And* just how did you intend to achieve it, in any case, sitting here stationary for the last hour or more?'

How could he have possibly known? She ran the tip of her tongue over lips that were now drier than they had been all day, and parried, 'Who says I have been?'

'Neil. He happened to see a stationary vehicle here, twice, while carrying out his last sweeps. . . and the reason we,' with a nod towards Bryan who had remained in the ute, 'came to investigate.'

Which also explained why they had been able to drive straight to her. Although it still didn't prevent her from declaring in some surprise, 'I didn't see or hear a helicopter.' She couldn't possibly have managed to get *that* close to the mustering area without realising it, could she? she despaired.

Court shrugged. 'Probably because he was just on treetop level, as well as a fair way downwind of you at the time.'

In view of the unrelieved, almost sweltering heat she had been experiencing, Eden wouldn't have thought there had been any breeze to be downwind of! 'Yes—well—I suppose it must have been while I was photographing the brumbies and wallabies,' she offered excusingly.

'You weren't photographing anything when we arrived, nor were you making any attempt to move. . . although your intention was to follow the truck out *this morning*, as I understand it,' he wasn't averse to reminding her in a deceptive drawl. Deceptive, because there was no sign of any laziness whatsoever in the compelling gaze that locked with hers immediately afterwards. 'There wouldn't be anything you're failing to disclose, by any chance, would there, honey?'

Eden caught her breath. Did he actually know, or was he just guessing? Either way, she suspected it wouldn't take much for him to become absolutely certain if that was the direction his thoughts were taking, and in a resultant about-face she abruptly abandoned her previous evasive approach in favour of a protective defiance.

'All right, so I lost sight of the tracks I was trying to follow, and then became hopelessly lost myself while attempting to find them again!' she flared. 'Who could blame me when the whole damned area is a mass of tyre marks leading in all directions! I tried listening for the helicopters, but I couldn't hear or see them anywhere. I also tried finding the track back to the homestead, but God only knows where that is!' with an acid grimace. She inhaled deeply, her tawny-gold eyes sparkling with a rebellious light. 'All of which just confirms your theory that I shouldn't be allowed outside the complex, I suppose!'

'Well, it sure doesn't do much for your claim that you should!' came the succinct return before Court unexpectedly headed back to the ute to say a few words to Bryan, extract a flask, and then return again as, with a wave, the overseer set off in a swirl of dust in the direction they had come.

Opening the driver's door of the Land Rover, Court handed her the flask. 'Here! I doubt you thought to bring anything to drink with you.' His accompanying words were voiced with a vexed irony, and immediately followed by the laconic command, 'Move over!'

His intention was plain, and although Eden did slide across to the passenger's seat, it was with a resentful reluctance. 'You didn't didn't have to take over,' she complained. It made her look and feel a total incompetent! 'I could have driven myself, if you'd just told me which direction I should go.'

Settling himself behind the wheel, Court pulled the door shut and flicked her an askance gaze as he switched on the engine. 'Yes, well, I'm sure you'll understand if I say. . . that would appear to be a rather debatable point right at the moment,' he mocked unsparingly.

Eden's cheeks warmed with a self-conscious heat, but since it wasn't a statement she could really contradict, she had little option but to content herself with a disdainful hunching of one shoulder. She had to admit, though, if only to herself, that she was surprised his reaction to her predicament hadn't been more trenchant, and even more surprised by his unanticipated consideration in even thinking to provide her with something to drink—which she now began to sample gratefully. If it had occurred to him at all, she would have thought him more likely to leave her thirsty, if only as a reminder that her dilemma had been one of her own making.

'So why didn't you use the map?' Court went on to enquire before moving off, and picking up the relevant sheet of paper on the seat between them. 'Joel apparently marked out the route for you.'

'Mmm, but unfortunately that wasn't of much help once I had no idea in which direction I was facing,' she defended herself with a trace of sarcasm. Didn't he think she'd at least *tried* to follow the younger man's directions?

'Not even when there's an arrow clearly showing North marked on it?' Court's own tone became more caustically pronounced.

'Well, what good was that when I'd lost *my* sense of direction?'

He gave a disbelieving shake of his head. 'Okay, then where was the sun?' he asked in shortening accents.

'In the sky, as usual,' she quipped with defensive glibness. 'Where else?'

'Where else?' he repeated on a rough note. 'Try to your right, to your left, in front of you, or behind you, unless you really do want to be confined to the complex from now on! God knows I'm beginning to wonder why, but I'm trying to help you avoid becoming lost again some time in the future! Or do you think that, just because the men seem to have taken a shine to you, they'd be only too willing to spend their time searching for you because *you're* too damned self-willed, or perverse, to make even the most basic observations regarding your surroundings!'

'No! That isn't it at all!' Eden protested vehemently, both dismayed and hurt that he could believe such a thing. 'And why *would* it occur to me that you might be trying to help me? It's always been the reverse before!' She paused, averting her gaze. 'I just thought you were attempting to—to rub in my stupidity for having got lost, and. . .' her voice lowered to a dismal whisper, 'I've already done that myself for the last five hours.'

Court expelled a heavy breath and rubbed a hand irritably around the back of his neck, his eyes never wavering from her downbent head and the attractively sculptured profile turned to him. 'You've really been here that long?' he asked quietly at length.

She pressed her lips together and nodded.

'You probably could have driven around the whole circumference of the area in that time.'

'I know,' she sighed. 'I even started to for a while, but I wasn't sure if the fuel would last that long if I attempted all of it—it looks so huge—and. . .' she swallowed hard, 'by then I wasn't certain I would recognise the track even if I did come across it. I presumed there are others leading from it too, so rather than take the chance on making another mistake and ending up goodness knows where, I decided it would be best to stay here. Then, if none of the mustering party had returned this way, at least Joel and Jim Stanley would have had some idea where I was likely to be.'

'Well, at least you showed *some* judgment there,' Court allowed, and Eden was surprised by the strength of the feeling of satisfaction that swept over her on having gained his approval, even if only in such a small way. No doubt because it was the first time ever, she deduced. 'So what did you think of Jim?' Court enquired after a slight pause.

'He was very helpful—and very sweet,' she relayed with the faint stirrings of a half-smile at the memory of the old man's attitude.

'Sweet!' He gave an obviously involuntary laugh of disbelief. 'Are you sure we're talking about the same person? He's a crusty old devil at the best of times, and the more so usually where women are concerned.'

Eden's head angled higher as she abruptly turned to look at him. 'Well, he wasn't to me,' she asserted resolutely. 'In fact, he even said I could call him by his first name, *and* that if I ever wanted any help again just to go and see him, because he'd been here for going on forty-six years and wouldn't steer me wrong.'

Briefly, thickly lashed aquamarine eyes studied her upturned features contemplatively, and then one corner of Court's shapely mouth took on a wry tilt and he shook his head. 'Well, well! So you've even managed to add his scalp to your collection, have you?' he drawled mockingly. 'You sure seem to have what it takes to win over the males on this damned property, don't you?'

Apart from you, that is, Eden added silently, despondently, then paused to wonder why she cared so much. Except for the fact that he was her employer, of course, she qualified swiftly.

'Well, if I have, it's not because that's what I deliberately set out to do,' she denied, subconsciously feeling the need to defend herself.

'Mmm, that's what makes it so bloody disturbing!' he growled suddenly, and turned away in an unexpectedly irritated movement. 'However, since it wasn't my intention to sit here discussing your numerous conquests of the opposite sex,' with more than a touch of sarcasm that Eden considered quite undeserved, 'I suggest we return our attention to the real reason for our being here.' He inhaled deeply. 'So for the second time. . . from which direction was the sun coming when you arrived here this morning?'

Eden caught nervously at her lower lip with pearly white teeth, and not only because she had no idea just what she had done wrong now to have caused such a change in his manner, but also because she was apprehensive of his reaction to the only answer she could give. She diffidently offered, 'I'm sorry, but I just don't know. I wasn't paying any attention to it.'

'Although you do know that it rises in the east, presumably?'

Indignation at his taunting tone began to dispel her nervousness. 'Yes, I do realise that,' she retorted on a sardonic note.

'Then it's a pity you didn't also realise that, with the north marked on it, you could therefore have worked out from this,' he tossed the map into her lap, 'in just which direction you *were* travelling, as well as the direction you needed to travel in order to retrace your route!'

Could she? Eden gazed at the piece of paper blankly at first, and then a little more closely as she attempted to work out just whereabouts the sun would have been. Then, going further, she made an effort to gauge from the present position of that now descending brilliant disc the procedure required for an afternoon return journey.

'You're saying the track I used this morning is. . . over *there*?' she gasped disbelievingly at last, pointing at an angle across the barren claypan. Had she really wandered so far off course?

'That's about the size of it,' Court confirmed, finally setting the Land Rover in motion and making for approximately where she had indicated. 'It may not be precise reckoning, but it will certainly set you in the general direction you want to go.' He flicked her an expressive glance. 'Difficult, wasn't it?'

Eden didn't trust herself to answer, but merely flushed and looked away, her eyes closing in despair. To think she had spent all that wasted time sitting in the heat when she could have both avoided making herself look a fool again, and probably could have reached the mustering point, even without any tyre marks to follow! It was enough to make her feel like crying—and she wasn't altogether surprised when a hot and stinging dampness did indeed make itself felt behind her closed lids a few seconds later. When all was said and done, she *had*, in succession, just suffered the two most ignominious days of her life!

Beside her, Court muttered something inaudible under his breath, and changed direction slightly, although it wasn't until the surface they were travelling on changed markedly some time later that Eden opened her eyes again to look about her with a frown as she noted that they were back among trees.

'This isn't the way I came this morning, is it?' she questioned doubtfully. She was certain it hadn't been this bumpy, or the vegetation quite so dense.

'No, it's a different route that cuts across the river further downstream,' she was advised in careless tones.

'And it's shorter,' she surmised flatly. It seemed the most logical reason when he was no doubt anxious to be relieved of her presence as soon as possible.

As if he sensed her thought processes, his firmly contoured lips shaped into a lazily whimsical smile, and her pulse raced erratically. 'As a matter of fact, it's slightly longer.' He paused, flexing a wide shoulder. 'I simply thought we might see something down here that you may be interested in photographing.'

Surprisingly, he appeared to be offering an olive branch, and Eden was only too willing to accept it, but made a determined effort to keep her relief and happiness at his unexpected, but welcome, change in demeanour from becoming too obvious, all the same, as she queried, 'For instance?'

'A couple of long-term residents,' he imparted blandly.

In other words, she was just going to have to wait
and see, Eden assumed, and took in the scenery
around her while she waited. Here, the path they followed was little more than a very rough track full of
rocks and deep ruts that had the vehicle lurching and
jolting from one to the other, the trees thicker and
more shading.

There were also numerous narrow waterways to
cross, smaller tributaries of the river, she supposed,
although when they reached it, she discovered Stockyard Creek to be much wider at that point, its banks
broad and thick with sand as it prepared to join the
waters of the Gulf.

Some distance away there was even an island of
sand in its centre, a couple of hardy trees tenaciously
clinging to life on it, and it was in this direction that
Court guided them until the track gradually petered
out in a long hollow behind the casuarina-studded
creek bank.

'Well, do you want to have a look first, or get your
camera ready?' He sent Eden an enquiring gaze as he
brought them to a halt and turned off the engine.

Eden's return glance was wry. 'Since I still don't
know what it is I've come to see, I think it had better
be the former.' Then, with a faint puckering of her
forehead, 'And how can you be sure they're there—
wherever that might be—anyway?'

'Because it's been possible to see them a couple of
times as we came along here,' Court smiled indo-
lently.

Disturbingly fascinated by the engaging sweep
catching at his mouth, Eden found it difficult to keep
her mind on the conversation. 'I—er—I didn't see
anything,' she pushed out shakily.

His smile widened to a knowing grin that did even less to help her retain her concentration. She was beginning to think it preferable when he wasn't being so tolerant! 'You probably did. . . but it just didn't register exactly what it was you were seeing.'

'Oh?' Her winged brows lifted in astonishment.

'Uh-huh!' he averred laconically, opening his door. His voice lowered to a murmur. 'But if you want to make certain you *do* see them, you'd better do exactly as I do, and very quietly at that, because the sound of our engine will already have made them just a little wary, in any case.'

Eden nodded, and following his example, made no attempt to shut her door again when she also alighted. Then she dogged his footsteps carefully as he made his way along the hollow for a short way before heading up the steep bank to lie full length in the sand in order to peer over the top from the concealment of a small bush instead of cresting the ridge.

'There! Next to those two logs on the island. Do you see them?' Court spoke so softly she could only just hear what he was saying.

Eden peered across the intervening water, sparkling brilliantly in the late afternoon sun—and gulped consulsively. He was right, she *had* seen them earlier, only she had thought they were merely more debris washed down the river during the wet just like the other logs. Now she realised that what she had really been seeing were two of the most monstrous-sized crocodiles she could ever have visualised! And having lived all her life in the north, she knew immediately that they weren't of the harmless variety either!

'Just how big are they?' she breathed eloquently without taking her eyes off the basking reptiles.

'At a guess I'd say about sixteen to seventeen, maybe even eighteen feet.'

She swallowed and swung to face him quickly. 'Are there many that size round here?'

He shook his head. 'No, there are quite a few smaller, of course, but they're the only two I've seen that large.' Pausing, Court quirked an enquiring brow. 'Worth capturing on film?'

'Oh, yes!' Her answer was unequivocal, and especially in view of the fact that she was well aware that, because of their shyness and subsequent preference for remaining under water while humans were about, it was normally very difficult to obtain photos of estuarine crocodiles in the wild. 'I'll just get my camera.' She promptly began edging back down the bank.

'Mmm, it probably won't be long now before they start slipping back into the water in order to look for some supper,' Court put forward drily.

Repressing a shudder, Eden sent him a speaking glance, although the thought of them disappearing was sufficient to stop her wasting time by commenting, and hurrying as rapidly and quietly as she could back to the Land Rover instead. In no time at all she had returned with an appropriately large lens in place, as well as a piece of towelling to rest the camera on and thereby prevent any sand from getting into it, because she didn't want to take the chance of scaring the crocodiles away by setting up a tripod.

'Well, at least that helped to make up for my otherwise wasted day,' she enthused spontaneously a few minutes later after having photographed the imposing subjects from a number of different angles. 'The light was catching them perfectly to prevent any shadows, and it was still bright enough to get a good depth of field too.' She turned to look at Court somewhat shyly. 'Thank you for showing them to me. They're really something!'

'Mmm, I thought you might appreciate them,' he owned idly.

'Oh, I did!' There was a slight hesitation. 'Even if I'm not quite sure why you'd bother to take the time to bring me here when I know how. . .' she bent her head, 'how irresponsible and stupid you think I've been, and—and that it was against your will that you allowed Alick to persuade you into agreeing to employ me at all.'

'Uh-uh!' He tilted her face up to his again. 'Against my better judgment, maybe, but not against my will, I can assure you, or you wouldn't now be employed here,' Court corrected wryly. 'As to the other. . .' his mouth assumed a rueful curve, his thumb moving absently against her chin, 'unthinking you may have been, but I doubt I'd ever consider you stupid. Besides, don't you think you deserved some compensation for having had an obviously lousy day?'

'I wouldn't have expected that thought to occur to you, though!' surprise had Eden exclaiming impulsively before she could put a halt to it.

'Yeah—well. . .' Court's lips twisted graphically. 'Be that as it may, it still gave me no pleasure to succeed in making you cry as well, nor is it a habit of mine to do so where females are concerned—believe it or not.'

Perhaps not intentionally, but at the same time she didn't doubt that over the years many a member of her sex would have shed tears over the undeniably prepossessing Court Buchanan, was Eden's first involuntary assessment. She gave herself a severe mental shake to dispel any such intrusive thoughts.

'So what makes you think you did manage to make me cry?' she parried. It made her feel oddly vulnerable for him to know he had the power to reduce her to tears.

He smiled lazily, provokingly. 'Just the fact that, closed eyes notwithstanding, there was more than a suspicion of wetness about those long lashes of yours.'

'Oh!' Eden pulled swiftly away from him, pushing herself into a sitting position. 'Well, even if I were, I'm sure you won't be letting it have a bearing on anything else,' she half accused, half sighed.

'Meaning?' Court eyed her intently as he levered himself up beside her.

She shrugged deprecatorily. 'Meaning, that even if I cried buckets of tears you still wouldn't change your mind about allowing me to actually *do* any tourist work!'

The corners of his eyes crinkled with sudden humour. 'I suppose I should have known it wouldn't be long before you got around to that again,' he drawled.

The notion that he found it amusing rankled, and had her lifting her head higher. 'And why wouldn't I?' she flared. 'It was the reason I was employed, or why I was *supposed* to be employed, wasn't it?'

'And you also know what *I* said in that regard. Finish taking your photos first.' He flicked a dark brow goadingly high. 'Or was all Alick's praise for your ability in that area just so much hot air, and you're now finding the task beyond you?'

'No, it's not beyond me!' Eden denied indignantly, suddenly discovering herself back on the defensive

again. 'It's just that—that I believed my taking photos was to be secondary to my other work, but as it
is. . .' She spread her hands helplessly, her topaz-
coloured eyes clouding as they lifted to his. 'I feel as
if I'm just here on sufferance, as if I'm a nuisance to
all concerned, and yet I was so looking forward
to. . .'

'Oh, for crying out loud, take over the hire of the
damn boats and vehicles then, if it means so much to
you!' Court interposed in tones of rueful exaspera-
tion.

'You don't have to do me any favours!' she
promptly retorted contrarily. 'Either you think I can
handle the work or. . .'

'Eden!' She was cut off once more by a roughen-
ing, disbelieving bark as Court dragged off his hat
and raked his fingers through his hair. 'Do you want
the work, or don't you?'

She hunched away from the question uncomfortably. 'Well—yes—of course. You know I do.'

'Then either accept it *now*, or I promise you it'll be
the last time I'll make such an offer! So what's it to
be?'

Eden pressed her lips together, her thoughts racing. She was being hard to please, she knew, and yet
she couldn't really have said why. After all, she was
getting what she wanted, and she surely hadn't
expected him to willingly surrender the work to her,
had she? No, she should just have been pleased—she
was pleased—to have had a victory of any kind in the
circumstances, and instead of fighting against it
should perhaps have even tried pushing her luck a little further. As Alick had claimed, she could hardly
be fired for attempting to do *more* work!

'I accept—thank you,' she relayed finally with a deliberately winning smile that she was gratified to note evidently caught him completely off guard. Lowering her lashes, she sent him an openly persuasive look from beneath their luxuriant, dusky length. 'As well, I could even ask around to find out who's interested in joining that shooting party you mentioned arranging yesterday, if you like.'

Court shook his head, an involuntary half-laugh issuing from his deeply tanned throat. 'Hell! I've heard of sudden about-turns, but this is ridiculous! You sure believe in the power of the unexpected, don't you, honey?'

If it succeeded in putting him off balance for a change, it was certainly one she would consider cultivating. 'Meaning you're agreeing?' She tried pushing home her advantage.

A lopsided grin that she found utterly, devastatingly beguiling caught at his firmly-defined mouth. 'Well, you're certainly persistent, I'll give you that,' he drawled.

Eden dimpled audaciously. 'While *you're* evading giving an answer!'

Momentarily, Court's startling blue-green gaze continued to hold hers, and then it gradually darkened as it dropped to the soft contours of her smiling mouth, abruptly sending prickles of awareness darting down her spine. 'And when you look like that, you're nothing short of unbelievably irresistible!' he growled huskily, and had reached out a hand to draw her towards him, his lips claiming hers compulsively, before she could even divine his intention, let alone forestall it.

Only by then it was too late, for as she had considered his mouth to be sexy in shape, Eden now found it even more so in practice, and capable of eliciting a response she was neither prepared for nor seemingly able to control. She tried to tell herself it was merely because of her prior pleased and relaxed attitude, but deep down she knew differently. She had been equally relaxed the night before when Nick kissed her, but she had experienced no such desire to respond with such disturbing willingness, no such warmth flooding through her then.

Now she seemed to have no mind of her own, only a wish to comply with the demands of Court's compelling mouth as it moved sensuously against hers, his tongue probing and exploring the sweet recesses her already parted lips made available to him, and was staggered by the feeling of disappointment that assailed her when the hand that had been cradling her head at last released her.

'I think it's time we were leaving,' Court proposed roughly, and jammed his hat cursorily back on his head.

Eden nodded, too confused and embarrassed by her ungovernable responses and unsettled emotions to look at him, and scurried to her feet in order to retrieve her camera. 'Yes, it's getting late,' she commented lamely and in stilted accents, but wanting to at least say something in the hope of appearing unaffectd by what had just occurred. It was beginning to seem she was no more immune to his vitally masculine brand of attraction than any of the other girls at Arrunga River!

Back in the Land Rover once more, Court turned to gaze meditatively at her carefully composed features for a few seconds before making any move to start the vehicle. 'I'm sorry,' he said heavily. 'It's not my normal policy to indulge in amorous interludes with members of my own staff.' His mouth shaped crookedly. 'As inappropriate a moment as it may seem to make such a claim.'

Not even with Crystal? Eden found herself wondering sceptically, inconsequentially, remembering what she had been told about that girl's endeavours. She forced her attention back to the immediate and shrugged with an assumed indifference. 'You don't have to worry, I wasn't intending to use it as some sort of lever to gain special consideration,' she gibed protectively.

'That wasn't what I was implying!' His repudiation was delivered in tightened tones.

'Then what was?' she countered impulsively, and much to her annoyance. She would really have much preferred to just let the matter drop. It had created too much disturbance within her already. 'That I shouldn't read anything into it because it was only a momentary lapse on your part?'

'*If* that's all it was,' he responded with a somewhat self-mocking nuance.

Eden caught her breath. Was he implying that it wasn't? In that case, and in view of her own feelings, she supposed she should have been gratified by the thought that he might not have been totally unsusceptible to her either, but somehow that inflection managed to produce a certain wariness instead. Consequently, her return was a defensively unconcerned, 'What else?'

Court didn't reply. He merely surveyed her with a probing but unrevealing gaze, before hunching a broad shoulder and turning to put the vehicle into motion.

For her part, Eden pretended to give her attention to the scene outside, although little of what she saw registered. There was only one thing on her mind, and that was the man beside her. . . and the perturbing effect he was starting to have on her emotions, particularly when he seemed to be giving the impression that he regretted the whole situation altogether!

CHAPTER SIX

DURING the next few weeks, now that she was actually allowed to at least begin to fulfil the position she had been hired for, Eden was able to gradually settle into the routine of the station and stop feeling quite so much the outsider.

Fortunately, due to the helpful information forwarded by Jim Stanley and Gaye Redman, she had managed to assume control over the hire of the boats and vehicles without any other embarrassing mishaps, and had even taken over the souvenir counter in the bar area as her own special domain. An incident that had drawn vociferous condemnation and vows of protest to Court from Crystal, but as his only reaction had been in the form of a sardonic glance on noting the appropriation—making Eden wonder if indeed Crystal had carried out her threat, after all—she had seen no reason to alter the arrangement.

Moreover, because the location was one where most visitors usually put in an appearance at some time of the day, especially new arrivals looking for a cold drink after their long, hot, and dusty journeys, and the fact that she had taken to wearing—originally, almost defiantly, but now automatically—the badge she had made and the property's T-shirts, she was also finding her assistance sought more and more on a variety of matters which would once have been directed towards Court.

Just how he viewed the situation she hadn't known until some time later. In truth, she hadn't really seen much of him at all since that disquieting day when she had been lost on the claypans, because his time seemed to have been fully occupied ever since with mustering, more trips with visitors to various areas of interest in the mini-bus the station maintained for just such purposes, and a number of other matters that kept him absent from the complex for the greater part of each day.

Late one afternoon, though, he had been using the radio when a family group had come seeking some information, and on the completion of his call he leant negligently against the counter, listening, as Eden responded to a request for information regarding fishing venues within walking distance of the homestead for the two young sons of the family.

'If you look at the map, you'll see that one of those waterways is marked as Saltwater Creek.' She pointed it out on the relevant material she had just provided them with. 'Well, that runs alongside that first line of trees behind here,' indicating the rear of the building with a wave of her hand this time. 'You'll find just about anywhere along there quite suitable. It's a mass of holes and snags—which is where the barramundi like to hang out, of course. There are plenty of other fish too, mind, such as black bream, perch, saratoga, and mangrove jack, although the latter are found closer to the tidal reaches of the river, naturally enough, But it's the barra you've really come for, I expect.' She smiled understandingly, and received enthusiastic nods all round in return.

'And if we took a boat out, could we also reach the. . . what's it called?' a quick search of the map by the boys' father ensued, 'the south arm from there?'

'Oh, yes,' she confirmed. 'That's Stockyard Creek. One's really as good as the other as a fishing venue, so what with the river itself as well further upstream before it divides, you can see there are plenty of areas to choose from.'

'And therefore no chance of them being fished out?'

'Not with almost two hundred miles of waterway to be fished, *and* a closed season on the barra later in the year when they're breeding. As you can see.'

Almost as if on cue a couple of other visitors chose that precise moment to mount the veranda at the other end of the room in order to proudly display their catch of three of the giant-sized fish they had strung on a pole which looked about to snap under the weight, and which the two men were obviously finding it hard work just to carry.

'Wow! Get a load of that, Dad!' exclaimed one of the boys, and immediately set off, along with his brother, to join the crowd admiring the delighted anglers' haul.

'Mmm, aren't they beauties! I can see what gear I'm going to have to unpack first if I'm going to get any peace,' the man turned to comment ruefully to Eden before he and his wife also made their way to the veranda.

With their departure, Court eyed her obliquely. 'Did you arrange to have those two appear like that?' he drawled on a lazy note.

'It was so opportune you'd think I did, wouldn't you?' she agreed with a laugh. 'But as a matter of fact the catches, over the last few days especially, have been quite spectacular. I'm sure everyone in the camping area must be eating fish for breakfast, lunch, and dinner. Even the lodge guests have been bringing them in for Norma to cook for them too.' Norma Willard was the restaurant's chef.

'Mmm, it's usually the same around this time of year,' he averred absently, his thoughts obviously elsewhere—as evidenced when he went on to probe, 'And just where did you come by all that information regarding the best areas to fish and the species available, etcetera, anyway?'

The fact that he queried it had Eden experiencing a sudden apprehension. Oh, lord, she hadn't fouled up something else after all, had she? 'Why? It was correct, wasn't it?'

'Very much so,' he owned drily, unaware of the feeling of sheer relief that surged through her as she heard him say so. 'That's why I asked. Because although you may have been able to pick up some of if from the brochures, you certainly couldn't have done so with all of it.'

'Yes, well, Jim's given me a few tips now and again, but mainly it was thanks to Alick on my first day here. Fortunately, *he* was prepared to pass on some information that might assist me,' she relayed with pointed sweetness.

'Well, I guess that was only to expected, wasn't it?' A faintly sardonic note entered Court's voice. Then, with a quizzically raised brow, 'Have you heard from him lately?'

She frowned in surprise. 'No. Should I have?'

'Maybe not,' he allowed with a shrug. 'I was forgetting.'

Forgetting what? she immediately frowned, perplexed.

'So what else have you been doing with your
time. . . apart from extolling the virtues of Saltwater and Stockyard Creeks, that is?' Court suddenly
continued in wry accents, making her start, and per-
force, dismiss her previous confused musing.

'Oh—er—this and that,' she evaded, nervously
recalling all those things she had done but which he
hadn't as yet actually given her permission to attend
to.

'Well, that was certainly specific,' he quipped,
mockery uppermost.

Eden flushed and hunched a deprecating shoulder.
'I didn't think you'd be interested in hearing every
minute detail.'

'Although *some* would be a trifle more enlightening, not to mention an improvement.' A hand lightly
spanning her chin tilted her head upwards. 'And
don't make the mistake of thinking I'm altogether
ignorant of just what goes on around here, huh?'

The warning wasn't lost on Eden and she swallowed, pulling away, and wondering just what he
seemed to be implying he did know, and why, if that
was the case, he hadn't seen fit to mention it previously. 'Yes—well—I finished taking the photographs
and sent them off, al-although I haven't received
them back as yet from the friend in Townsville who
does my developing and printing for me.' She paused,
debating as to just what she should divulge next.

'And the chopper flights?' Court cursorily made
the decision for her.

'Oh, those,' she acknowledged with a somewhat
sickly half smile. 'Well, yes, I did—er—arrange a
couple one afternoon after Nick and the others had
returned from working on Summerhill. You weren't

around at the time,' she hurried to explain, 'but since it was both couples' last day here and they were so keen to go—plus Nick saying that they often provided such flights over the area—I didn't want to disappoint them, so I—I simply put them in touch with Nick and Larry and they took it from there.' She hastened to add, 'And to everyone's satisfaction, evidently, judging by the comments made when they returned.'

'Hmm. . .' She was subjected to an intent, darkly fringed blue-green gaze that betrayed nothing. 'So don't stop there. Let's have the rest of it.'

Vexedly beginning to suspect he already damned well knew the rest of it, Eden expelled a resigned breath and listed them briskly. 'I arranged a four-day camp-out trail ride for a group of seven; I organised it so that some others could view and participate in one of the ground musters; I also arranged for a wildlife safari out to the claypans and beyond as well as for more mounts to be brought in to the horse paddock for those just wanting to go for shorter rides.' There was a slight hesitation before she went on even more swiftly, 'I personally drove in to collect a couple requiring transport from the airstrip in Torrington. For the last couple of days people have started handing their camping fees to me. And today I accepted a booking: the letter of confirmation I typed is on your desk awaiting your signature.'

Court uttered a disbelieving expletive, and it was only then that Eden realised he *hadn't* been fully aware of all she had undertaken, and she began chewing at her lip nervously, wishing she hadn't been quite so expansive.

'Hell! When Bryan's said some of the men have been working elsewhere, I've assumed it was at his direction, not yours!' he bit out.

'I—I did check with him first to see if—if. . .'

'Oh?' he interposed expressively. 'And why him and not me, eh? Because you knew what the result would be if you did? Or wasn't I here when all that was taking place either?' He raised a sardonic brow.

Eden shifted her stance restlessly. 'S-sometimes you were,' she confessed with a stammer, and hurried on excusingly, 'But mostly you were already very busy, and—and I was only trying to help.'

'Make me redundant, more like!' retorted Court, but in more drily resigned tones of long-suffering than infuriated ones, giving Eden cause to sigh in relief.

'On, no, I couldn't ever do that,' she denied earnestly, chancing a whimsical half-smile. 'I receive too many questions—that I'm afraid I just haven't learnt all the answers to as yet—about the property itself and the cattle, and so on, for that ever to happen.'

His lips twitched wryly. 'Well, I guess it's something to know I haven't been made completely superfluous. But. . . such as?'

'Oh, all sorts of things. Like, how long your family have been here. . .' She ventured to send him a partly expectant, partly hinting glance from beneath the curtain of her lashes.

Momentarily, he simply returned her gaze unwaveringly, then he gave a rueful half laugh and told her, 'Since the eighteen-nineties.'

Encouraged, Eden pressed on. 'Why you use more than one brand. Apparently a few of them were watching some more of the cattle being branded and dipped in the yards last week and noticed different ones were used.'

There was a short pause, and then, 'Without going into too much detail, in order to separate the breeders from the rest, mainly. Although we do also use a different brand for the horses as well.'

She nodded. 'I've even had. . . what exactly are Droughtmasters, and why do you run them in preference to other breeds?'

'What are they?' Court's eyes lifted skywards eloquently. 'Well, if you really want to get technical. . . they're a three-eighths to five-eighths—ours are five-eighths—Brahman-Shorthorn cross which was evolved in Queensland to suit the tropics. They do also still have some Hereford characteristics from experimentation in the early days, but this is now being bred out. Why do we prefer them? Because they're more resistant to both ticks and internal parasites, they withstand the heat far better, they're less susceptible to blight, and even more important, when the grass is losing its nutrition at the end of the dry season they process it more efficiently.' His mouth shaped sardonically. 'Anything else?'

'Actually, the list is almost limitless,' Eden smiled, but didn't press the matter in view of already having done better than she had expected. 'In fact it's quite incredible at times just what people do want to know. However, I'm pleased to say that, thanks to Jim's assistance, I do now know a lot of the bird species that frequent the area, and can at last distinguish a carbeen from a ghost gum,' accompanied by a rueful laugh, 'as well as recognise a number of the other trees present.' She gave her head an amused shake. 'It never occurred to me that anyone would be wanting to know what trees you had here.'

'You wait until they get on to the grasses and the wildflowers,' he mocked lazily.

Her eyes widened. 'Those too?' Then, with a suspect look of innocent regret, 'Oh, well, since you're evidently averse to me providing too much assistance, I suppose I shall just have to re-direct all those enquiries to you, shan't I?'

Court shook his head in leisurely veto. 'Uh-uh! Oh, no you don't, honey!' He bent his head lower, his even white teeth beginning to show in a taunting smile that had Eden wrestling for control of her suddenly chaotic senses. 'You claimed to have wanted to take charge of all tourist activities, and you've certainly done your best in that regard this last week or more, so now you can just get on with it.'

'You mean, you're actually saying I *can* make all the arrangements from now on?' Eden held her breath, unable to believe she had heard correctly. It definitely wasn't the outcome she had anticipated when he had started his questioning.

For a time there was no reply as he slowly surveyed her hopeful features, and then his mouth slanted crookedly. 'It would seem like it,' he conceded, but on such a heavily exhaled note that she wondered if he really would have preferred it otherwise, and it therefore took some of the gloss from her pleasure.

Reaching out a tentative hand, she stopped before it actually contacted his arm. 'You don't have to agree to it if—if you'd really rather not,' she offered helplessly.

'So why should I make this time an exception?' he countered with satiric humour. 'I seem to have done nothing *but* accede to suggestions I haven't been in agreement with ever since you arrived!'

Eden dropped her gaze. 'I'm sorry. I really wasn't meaning to. . .'

'Forget it, honey!' Court interrupted to instruct roughly, and when she looked up it was to see him running a hand wearily around the back of his neck. 'It's not your fault. I guess I'm just having difficulty reconciling myself to the irreconcilable.'

Her forehead creased with a frown. 'I don't follow you.'

'Well, maybe I should be thankful for that at least,' he quipped, but no less cryptically than with his original remark as far as Eden was concerned. 'But in the meantime,' he continued, his expression turning rueful, 'I reckon I could do with a drink. It's been a long, hot, and somewhat trying day.' With a faint dip of his head he turned to make for the bar.

Eden watched dejectedly as he seated his lithe figure on one of the leather-topped stools, her gaze unconsciously becoming even more wistful when, with a coquettish smile, who else but Crystal hastened to serve him and engage him in blandishing conversation. That the dark-haired girl should also spare her a smirk of triumph as she turned to extract a can from the row of fridges behind her only caused her spirits to sink lower.

Having finally succeeded, as Alick had forecast, in forcing his stepbrother by one means or another into finally accepting her as Tourist Manager, she would have expected to be feeling pleased—but she wasn't. Court's unanticipated reaction had seen to that. Now she merely found herself wishing the position could have been offered to her, and reluctant to even accept it now because of the manner in which it had been granted.

A covert look across to the bar showed Crystal still monopolising Court's attention, and her own time, leaving Gaye to do the majority of the work—something that had the younger girl sending an expressive grimace in Eden's direction on catching her eye, and which Eden tried to respond to as naturally as possible. The two of them had been on quite friendly terms for some time now. As, in fact, Eden had been with all the other members of the staff as well. Apart from Crystal, of course, who seemed to consider it beneath her dignity to associate with most of them.

When no other visitors appeared to require her services, though, Eden was glad to take the opportunity to leave the confines of the bar and be on her own for a while to get her thoughts back on course once more. So in reply to Nick's signal that she join him and Joel, she gave a regretful gesture pretending she had work elsewhere to conclude, and slipped out the back way.

Outside, the appetising aroma of spit-roasted beef, together with the sight of the kitchen and dining-room staff beginning their other preparations for the evening's meal at the long wooden tables on the grass beside the swimming pool as she passed, reminded her that it was Saturday night. It was the one evening of the week when just about everyone on the station came together to share their meal and experiences, and have a good time.

Only unlike the previous occasions, this time Eden didn't really feel in the mood for any such get-together and decided she would rather watch the latest video that someone had brought from town instead. With no television reception, videos had provided a popular substitute in the bush and were usually shared among everyone on the property.

On reaching the homestead, she leant on the veranda rail to watch as the sun made its nightly descent into the waters of the Gulf, turning them gold, and orange, and blood-red as it did so, and then she wandered moodily inside to collect a cold drink from the fridge in the kitchen before settling herself in a comfortable chair in the sitting-room with a volume on native birds that she had taken from a well-endowed bookshelf. Unaccountably, now that she had the peace and quiet to dissect and rearrange her troubled thoughts, she found herself deliberately procrastinating.

She was still there some considerable time later when the sound of booted feet mounting the steps two at a time disrupted her concentration—not that she had managed to assimilate much of what she had read, in any case—and she looked up just as Court came to a sudden halt on seeing her as he made to pass the room. The speed with which he had taken the steps had made it evident he was in a hurry. The fact that his shirt had already been pulled free of his jeans, and that he was even at that moment undoing the last of the buttons, simply confirmed his urgency. . . and made Eden intensely aware of the muscular, mahogany-coloured flesh now visible.

'What in blazes are you doing here?' he immediately demanded in surprise.

Repressing the facetious, and defensive, 'I live here!' that sprang to her lips, Eden raised a diffident shoulder and settled for the obvious. 'I'm reading.'

'I can see that!' Court retorted. 'But you seem to have forgotten, this happens to be Saturday night.' Shades of mockery entered his voice.

So that was what had prompted the question. 'Yes, well, I thought I might give the barbecue a miss tonight.'

'Oh, did you?' His brows peaked significantly as he began moving into the room. 'Then I suggest you reconsider, honey, because one of the reasons for putting on these Saturday night barbecues was to provide an opportunity when most of the staff are available for people to ask any questions they want, and since you happen to be the person in charge of tourist activities. . .'

'No, I'm not!' Eden inserted, in a rush, partly because of her denial having formed almost without conscious volition, and partly before she got cold feet.

'What do you mean. . . no, you're not?' His eyes narrowed as his hands thumped to rest on lean hips, the action parting his shirt further so that even more of his powerful frame was uncovered.

She drew a deep breath. 'I—I'd rather not have the position if you don't feel able to—to actually offer it to me,' she just managed to get out.

'Offer it?' Court's expression assumed an ironic cast. 'It was given to you!'

'Precisely!' Her voice rose slightly. 'In resignation. . . not approbation!'

'So what are you suggesting? That I get down on my knees and humbly beg you to. . .'

'I didn't say that!'

'Then be satisfied you got it at all! It wasn't my intention that you should, believe me!'

'You didn't have to tell *me* that!' Eden flared with a hint of bitterness in her tone.

A nerve tensed in Court's cheek, the glittering look in his eyes as he leant down to place his hands on the arms of her chair abruptly making her realise that he'd obviously had more than that one drink at the bar, although he just as evidently wasn't drunk. It simply gave him a darkly dangerous air that set her pulse thudding and had her breath catching in her throat apprehensively.

'In that case, you've no reason to complain, have you? As I said earlier, you wanted the job. . . now do it!' he ordered with a snap.

'All right, I will!' Her tawny-gold eyes clashed militantly with his for a moment, then she sighed despairingly. 'I just wish I knew why you feel about it as you apparently do.'

Court uttered a short, derisive laugh and pushed himself upright once more. 'No one can play dumb to *that* extent, honey!' he scorned sarcastically. 'And you're wasting time. So why don't you just get a move on, instead of being so damned difficult, huh?' He returned on his heel to begin striding away.

Her, difficult! Eden gasped, glaring after him indignantly. And just what did he think he was, when one minute he would treat her with a disarming indulgence, and the next with bewildering irritation! Moreover, just what had he meant, anyhow, by implying she had been playing dumb? Because he'd made no secret of his being in favour of hiring a Tourist Manager in the first place?'

But surely, just the fact that he *had* handed all such activities over to her—even if grudgingly—discounted that contention. Or was it that he just didn't like having been proved wrong, in that he obviously could do with assistance in that area? Somehow she didn't think so, but at the same time, if that wasn't the reason, then what was? Baffled, she shook her head in confusion and rose to her feet, her thoughts remaining introspective as she made ready for the barbecue she would much rather not have attended.

By the time Eden put in an appearance at the large
gathering beside the pool, a number of those present
were already partaking of their meals. Others were
helping themselves to a variety of foods laid out on
the serving tables, still more standing in groups, or
moving from one to the other, talking and drinking.

Court, who had left the house before her, she
noted, was in conversation with a tour leader and
some of his passengers from a coach that arrived that
morning. Joel, Nick, and the other helicopter pilots,
as well as the station's ringers, also proved popular
targets for interestedly enquiring visitors. As she soon
found herself to be also, although in her case with
someone she would have preferred to avoid.

'Ah, there you are! I've been looking out for you,'
said an unctuous male voice uncomfortably close to
her ear, a heavy hand sliding familiarly around her
slender waist. 'I thought we might have dinner
together, just the two of us.'

Eden extricated herself swiftly from the fingers that
had a discomfiting tendency to clutch, and turned to
face the man with a forced, polite smile. Heavy-set
and heavy-featured, with somewhat small, knowing
eyes that looked out from beneath thick brows in a
face that perhaps twenty-odd years before may have
had some claim to being good-looking, Des Porter
with his three companions, had arrived the previous
day, but since which time, to Eden's discomfort, she
had been all too conscious of his unwelcome gaze
following her every move whenever she happened to
be in his vicinity.

'I'm sorry, Mr Porter. . .'

'Des,' he corrected with an ingratiating smile.

'Mr Porter,' she reiterated resolutely, despite
informality being the norm where most visitors were

concerned. 'I'm sorry, but I'll have to decline. On Saturdays, in particular, the staff are expected to mix with everyone here.' She began edging away.

He caught at her arm to stop her. 'Then how about a drink afterwards?'

'It's usually time for the bar to close too once we've finished here,' she parried, trying to ease herself free once more, but unsuccessfully on this occasion.

'There's always our lodge,' he proposed, gesturing briefly towards his companions who were already eating. 'We're not down in the camping area, you know. And. . .' he smiled again—or leered, was more like it, in Eden's estimation—and slid his hand up and down her arm in a faintly suggestive movement, 'with the few tinnies we've got on ice, we could have ourselves a good time.'

Was he kidding? Not that she was meaning to cast aspersions on the other three men with him, who all appeared quite likeable—and content to restrict themselves to the activities that *were* on offer! 'No, I don't think so, thank you, Mr Porter,' Eden refused slightly less civilly than previously. 'Now, if you have no questions to ask regarding Arrunga River. . .' She started pulling against his grasp quite openly this time.

'Oh, but I'm sure there must be some I could think of,' he pounced on the excuse swiftly. 'So why don't we. . .'

'Come on now, Eden, you're supposed to be circulating, not just reserving your attention for one person. . .however much you may like to,' came the rebuking interruption from Crystal as she wove her way between the crowd with a tray of drinks, but thereby providing the distraction necessary for Eden to at last regain her freedom. A pseudo-bantering smile was turned in Des Porter's direction. 'All the men are keen on our little Tourist Manager. She's making quite a name for herself, in fact. None the less, the boss would prefer it if she kept her mind on what she was supposed to be doing once in a while, of course, and right at the moment work calls. So sorry, Des, you'll just have to excuse her until some other time.' She gave Eden a sharp push in the back to ensure that the younger girl remained in front of her as she resumed walking.

Thankful though she was for Crystal's intervention, Eden still wasn't prepared to allow her construction of the incident to go unchallenged, however. 'I can assure you I wasn't encouraging him, Crystal!' she protested. 'Just the opposite, as it happens. I was trying to get away from him!'

'Oh, sure. . . once you saw me coming!' Crystal retorted. 'But before that you certainly didn't seem to have any objection to him pawing you!'

'Because I was trying to be diplomatic, and not cause a scene!'

'Oh, don't give me that! Your type's always the same—if they're male, you're interested! Do you think I haven't seen you playing up to all the men here? I understand you've even got that foul-tempered, stupid old goat, Jim Stanley, infatuated with you as well! God, it's sickening!' A disparaging sneer contorted Crystal's features. 'Not that I suppose we should have expected any better from someone like you. . . as I was saying to Court only this afternoon!'

Eden inhaled sharply. 'And just what's that supposed to mean?' she demanded, wondering if it could also have been that reason for Court's behaviour when he had returned to the homestead.

Crystal gave a disdainful laugh, her dark eyes narrowing to mere slits. 'As if you don't know!' she snorted, and turned to the relevant table to begin serving the drinks, leaving Eden to digest her words in frowning bewilderment.

For the second time now in as many hours she had been accused of equivocating, and she was still no wiser to the reason. So just *what* was she supposed to have done? Made no secret of the fact that she had wanted the position of Tourist Manager and had done everything in her power to see that she got it—in spite of all resistance? She shook her head. No, it had to have been as a result of just another of Crystal's malicious attempts to denigrate her—as she also did to almost everyone else on occasion—becauseshe had always been against her being hired, Eden reasoned. Beginning to breathe a little easier, she gave a dismissive shrug and made her way over to the table where Nick and Joel were preparing to have their meal.

The remainder of the evening passed relatively uneventfully for Eden as she had her own dinner in company with a number of visitors, the questions put to her becoming more desultory as time wore on, although one particular query, late in the night, did manage to stump her completely.

'How come the tides never seem to change much round here?' asked a couple who she knew to be extremely keen on their fishing. 'We've gone out into the Gulf for the last three days and it's high when we leave and not much different when we return.'

'Isn't it?' was her initial surprised response. Then, when no ready answer presented itself, she continued with a half-laugh, 'Yes, well, I think I'd—er—better check that one out for you.' She looked round for someone else to ask.

When the only person available within distance proved to be Court, she hesitated before calling him over. Since their altercation in the homestead she had been nervously conscious of his taut presence—and the fact that he appeared to have deliberately avoided any contact with her—and so her eventual signal was somewhat halfheartedly made, and his subsequent approach viewed warily.

'Doreen and Lyle were just asking why the tides in the Gulf don't appear to change much,' she relayed immediately, and in something of a hurry, as soon as he joined them. She lifted a deprecating shoulder. 'I'm afraid I didn't know the answer.'

'Hmm. . . I thought it must have been something unusual to have you voluntarily seeking my advice,' he drawled with the barest hint of mockery evident— which she hoped went undetected by the others— before addressing himself to the married couple. 'However, the reason for that slow movement—apart from the fact that our ebb tides happen to be occuring at night at the moment—is that this particular part of the Gulf only has one tide a day, not two, as in other places. Well, at least, normally only one, that is.' The addition was imparted with an oblique smile. 'When there's a new moon, we get a mixture of both. For instance, next month there'll be two tides on the first day, one tide the following day, and then two tides for the next two days, after which it will revert to all single tides once again until the next new moon.'

Lyle nodded his acknowledgement. 'So that's it. I have heard of such occurrences, but I must admit I didn't realise this was one of those areas where they took place.'

'While I haven't even heard of it,' put in his wife ruefully. 'Having lived all my life on a coast where they do always have two tides, I automatically assumed everywhere else did as well.'

'Well, you're not on your own there,' Court advised on a wryly humorous not. 'We've had a considerable number of visitors over the years who've been caught in the same way.'

'Well, at least that makes me feel a little better,' laughed Doreen.

'It doesn't make me feel quite so bad either,' Eden confessed spontaneously once the couple had departed. 'Because I thought the same as she did, too.' She paused, and then cast Court a diffident glance. 'Thank you for helping me out.'

He shrugged impassively. 'It's all part of the business.'

'Yes, of course,' she agreed quickly. She didn't want him thinking she was under the impression that it might have been for any other reason that he had responded to her signal. 'I can see there's still a lot I have to learn about Arrunga River.'

'Well, don't lose any sleep over it. I'm sure you'll manage to succeed in that as you have in everything else.' The prediction was made in hard-edged tones that had Eden's finely arched brows drawing together in a frown.

'Court. . .' She put out a hesitant hand—and jumped involuntarily when an arm abruptly descending on to her shoulders heralded Nick's untimely appearance.

'So how's my favourite girl going?' he enquired blithely, and all unaware or her slight wince of self-consciousness on noting the tightening set of Court's strong features at the younger man's proprietorial attitude. 'I've hardly seen you all evening.'

'Yes—well—we've all been busy,' she murmured uncomfortably, wishing he hadn't joined them, and with her eyes remaining surreptitiously fixed to Court's taut face. 'There really hasn't been much time for—for anything else.'

'Although that's about to change, let's hope,' Nick proposed with a grin. 'How about coming and having a drink with me?'

Eden moved restively. 'I—er. . .'

'Why don't you join us too, Court?' Nick went on to suggest. 'No doubt you could do with one as well.'

'Not at the moment, thanks all the same,' Court declined brusquely. 'In fact, if you'll excuse me. . .' He gave a brief nod and started to take his leave.

'Mmm, I can't say I blame him for preferring *her* company to ours,' Nick laughed expressively, watching the direction in which the other man headed.

'Whose?' demanded Eden immediately, and more sharply than she intended as she sent a searching look after Court.

'Why, the slashing brunette who's almost wearing that low-cut red dress, naturally!' He laughed again. 'Don't tell me you haven't noticed her! She's been making it obvious all evening just where her interest lies.'

'Oh!' Eden was shocked by the feelings of animosity that suddenly surged through her, *and* even more stunned when they fused with an uncustomary but burning jealousy as she watched the girl in question press herself close to Court's side and gaze up at him invitingly as he joined the group she was with.

'I—er—suppose he attracts a lot of that sort of thing,' she commented, endeavouring not to sound as waspish as she felt.

'You can say that again!' Nick's confirmation was wryly made and explicit—and not at all appreciated. 'Even I can see that he's certainly got something that appeals to the opposite sex, and being the boss of the place as well just makes him that much more of a magnet, I guess.' His lips twitched ruefully, and with a certain tolerant envy.

'Yes—well . . .' Eden resolutely turned her back on the scene that had caused such an unexpected upheaval within her emotions, and forced a smile on to her lips. 'Now what about that drink you promised me?'

None the less, in spite of her ensuing efforts to ignore what was happening at that one particular, not far distant table, and to concentrate all her attention on her companion, Eden eventually had to concede that she was fighting a losing battle. Consequently, pleading a headache, she made her apologies to Nick and, refusing his offer to walk with her back to the homestead, set off to seek her bed. As a number of the visitors were also beginning to do.

Leaving the brightly lit pool area, she made her way along the sandy path with her head bent contemplatively, and as a result it wasn't until she almost collided with another figure in the shadows created by a strongly perfumed frangipani that she realised there was anyone else about.

'I'm sorry,' she apologised mechanically even before she'd finished looking up. 'I must have been lost in thought.'

'About me?' hazarded Des Porter hopefully.

Grimacing on recognising him, Eden was in no mood to be as tactful as she had tried to be earlier. 'Hardly!' she retorted in pungent accents and made to move past him.

He promptly moved to bar her path again, and caught her by the shoulders with heavy hands. 'Now you know you really don't mean that,' he chuckled imperviously. 'Even Crystal could tell that.'

With an inward curse for both him and Crystal, Eden made an effort to push his hands away. 'Mr Porter. . .'

'Des,' he contradicted just as he had previously, and to her dismay began drawing her closer. His eyes darkened as they roamed avidly over her face, making her skin crawl. 'God, I could feast my eyes on you for ever! Where have you been all my life?'

Was he for real? 'I wasn't alive for the first half of it!' she quipped on a snubbing note, and started to struggle in earnest. 'Now kindly take your damned hands off me, and. . .'

'Then just think of all I'll be able to teach you,' he cut in fervently as if she hadn't spoken, and lowering his head towards hers even as he pulled her further into the shadows.

Eden gasped, actually becoming alarmed for the first time, and twisted her face wildly away from his as she hit out at him with her clenched fists. Then she was stumbling backwards in surprise relief on feeling the brawny arms releasing their grip as her attacker abruptly staggered a couple of steps away from her with a grunted exclamation.

'I think you're being told your attentions are unwelcome, *mate*!' Court's sarcastically biting voice sounded out of the darkness as he continued to yank the other man's head back by a handful of hair.

'Gawd! You're breaking me bloody neck!' Des Porter growled irately, his thoughts evidently concerned with the immediate only.

In one swift movement, Court relinquished his grip and, swinging him round, shoved him back against the trunk of the tree with a hand flat against his chest, and a force that had them all being showered with fragrant apricot-coloured blossoms. 'Don't tempt me!' he grated. 'There's nothing I'd like better! And if it wasn't for the other three with you, you'd be getting your marching orders here and now!'

'Oh, yeah!' came the half challenging, half blustering sneer as Des Porter eyed his younger, taller, more muscular, and obviously fitter adversary. 'And what business is it of yours if one of your staff fancies a little bit on the side, eh? I notice you don't seem averse to some of the same with that little trollop in red!'

A description Eden was ashamed to realise pleased her no end.

Court took a threatening step forward. 'Except that, in your case, it evidently *wasn't* Eden who had anything of the sort in mind!'

'She was just teasing, that's all!' scoffed Porter, and Eden gasped.

'I was not!' she intervened to protest hotly.

He continued as if she hadn't spoken, his eyes narrowing. 'And maybe *you*. . .' glancing savagely at Court, 'won't be feeling so cocky either when I lay a charge against you for assault when I get back to town!'

'Be my guest!' invited Court on a ominous note. 'Because it will be my pleasure to counter with one

for your having molested one of my staff! Which I've
no doubt your *wife* will find most enlightening when
she hears of it!'

That last remark obviously struck home, for the
other man's demeanour altered rapidly. 'I—well—
there's no need for you to get all vindictive about it,'
he charged, but somewhat more agitated than defiant
now. 'There was no harm done, and—and I was only
having a bit of fun, after all.

Court uttered a disparaging sound deep in his
throat. 'Fun that was neither appreciated nor is tol-
erated here! And I give you fair warning. . . if I see
you so much as even speaking to Eden again, I won't
give a damn about the others with you—you'll find
yourself thrown off this property before you know
what's hit you!'

'But—but she handles the tourist activities! How
can I explain to me mates why. . .'

'I couldn't care less! You created the problem—
now you solve it! Just get out of my sight before I
change my mind!'

After a slight hesitation, as if he would have liked
to say more regardless, the older man did as directed,
albeit with something like a rancorous, but smoth-
ered, snarl as he pushed past them.

Free of his unwanted and unpleasant presence at
last, Eden released a relieved breath and glanced
upwards self-consciously. 'Thank you for coming to
my assistance for the second time this evening,' she
said with a half-smile that quickly came and went.

Court acknowledged her gratitude with a deprecating flexing of one shoulder. 'I suspected he might
have been giving you trouble earlier, so when he hurried off in the direction of the homestead,

immediately you looked like leaving, I thought it might be as well for me to follow.'

'Well, I'm certainly glad you did,' she owned sincerely, and unable to suppress the wayward feeling of almost malicious satisfaction that flooded through her on realising that he apparently hadn't been so engrossed with the brunette to take note of what else was happening, particularly with regard to herself.

He eyed her meditatively. 'So how do you feel, anyway?'

'Still a little shaky, I guess. I was just so unprepared.'

Court drew a deep breath. 'Do you want me to get Nick?'

'What for?' Her eyes widened in surprise.

'Comfort,' he proposed flatly.

'Oh!' She looked away swiftly, suddenly realising that it was only his comfort, only him, she wanted. 'No, I don't think so,' she declined quietly.

'I'll walk you the rest of the way, then,' he offered in impassive tones, turning in the appropriate direction.

Eden swallowed miserably, her previous sense of gratification having totally dissipated. She had merely been fooling herself if she believed it had been anything but a sense of duty that had made him follow her! 'You don't have to if—if there's something else you would rather be doing,' she faltered.

'It can wait!' Court returned with unexpected curtness, and cupping her elbow, began impelling her along the path beside him.

Anticipating him leaving again as soon as they reached the bottom of the steps, Eden was surprised when he mounted them with her and, in fact, didn't remove his impersonal but still warmly disturbing touch until they had entered the house and he switched on the sitting-room lights.

'You'll be all right?' he enquired tersely.

She managed a meagre nod, a painful lump sticking in her throat at the thought of him leaving.

'You're sure?' An inexorable hand tilted her face upwards, the note of sudden concern in his voice her undoing as her gaze was forced to connect with his frowning features.

Eden ran her tongue over her lips helplessly. 'Do you—have to go. . . right away?' she breathed unsteadily.

'Meaning?' Court's darkly framed eyes locked watchfully with hers.

She took a long, ragged breath and hunched a slender shoulder. 'Would it be asking too much, and—and so impossible, for you to—perhaps stay and talk for just—a little while?'

He gave a harsh mirthless laugh. 'Except that, where you're concerned, talking isn't what my instincts feel inclined to engage in, unfortunately!'

Tension suddenly seemed to vibrate in the air between them and Eden's breathing quickened. 'They don't?'

'No!' He swung away sharply, then inhaling deeply turned back again to declare in heavy tones, 'And you're just suffering a reaction to what happened. You should have let me fetch Nick.'

'I didn't want Nick,' she blurted.

'Then you should have!'

Because despite what he had said, he would still rather return to the girl in red? Tears threatened, and Eden bent her head low. 'Of course,' she murmured with a throatiness she couldn't control. 'I'm sorry to have detained you, then. I should have known you wouldn't want. . . that I was the last person. . .' She broke off, aware she was in danger of becoming incoherent, and about-turning, rushed from the room.

'Eden!' she heard Court call in partly exasperated, partly despairing accents behind her, and before she could reach her bedroom a hand settling on the nape of her neck brought her to a halt. 'For God's sake. . .!' He spun her round to face him, his expression becoming strained as he took in the suspicious brightness of her eyes. 'I'm sorry,' he apologised in gruff tones. 'You haven't had a very pleasant evening, and I haven't exactly done much to help, but. . .' he paused, his gaze darkening as it came to rest on her soft lips, '... oh, God, what am I going to do about you?' He pulled her roughly into his arms, his mouth capturing hers with a fiery desire.

CHAPTER SEVEN

ALTHOUGH Court's wording might have been somewhat puzzling, his actions were anything but, and
Eden promptly responded to them accordingly. A
short time earlier she had realised that it was only his
comfort, his presence, she had wanted, and now she
knew why. She loved him—beyond belief! In fact, she
couldn't bear to even contemplate what life without
him again might even be like, and as a result she
wound her arms about him tightly, never wanting to
let him go.

A wave of heat consumed her as his tongue sought
hers, stirring hitherto unknown emotions that made
her tremble. His hands moved slowly down her back,
urging her even closer, so that she was immediately
aware of his hard, muscular length pressing so
demandingly against her own. Then, with a smoth-
ered sound of helplessness, he dragged his mouth
from hers and, picking her up in his arms, carried her
swiftly into her bedroom.

Gently, he set her down on the bed, his lean and
powerful body soon following, and she felt her pulse
race as he drew her back into his arms, his lips claiming hers once again with a sensuous passion that
made her head spin. Deep within, she moaned softly
as his hands caressed her and his mouth began a tan-
talising exploration of her cheeks, her eyes, her
slender throat, and the wildly palpitating hollow at
its base.

Filled with an aching desire, Eden slid her hands
beneath his silk knit shirt, her fingers moving exper-
imentally from his lithe waist to his smooth, teak-
dark, muscle-ridged back and then, after he had
swiftly shrugged out of the garment, to the broad
expanse of his chest. He had the steel-honed body of
a man of action and she relished the feel of its hardness beneath her fingertips.

Giving a convulsive shudder at the touch of her
roaming hands, Court set his mouth to the warm
hollow of her shoulder, his tongue stroking the soft
skin exposed by her sun-frock, his hand finding the
large buttons of its front fastening and the clasp of
her bra underneath. Almost before his action could
register, her full breasts were bared to his ardent gaze,
and she quivered as his fingers leisurely explored the
firm, satin-smooth flesh, and skilfully teased her
already swollen nipples until she thought she could
stand the exquisite pleasure no longer. Although only
until his mouth followed the course of his hands,
licking and sucking, whereupon she arched against
him feverishly, her fingers entwining within his dark
hair, her body aflame, and was unable to withhold
the sob of pure ecstasy within her.

Neither of them heard Joel enter the house, their
first and only hint of his presence being the drily bantering quip, 'Don't you two worry about it, I'll turn
the lights off!' Which was followed by total darkness
as the sitting-room lights were indeed doused and he
made his way along the passageway to his own room.

Embarrassment immediately washed over Eden at
his not only having obviously deduced what was taking place in her room, but worse, that he might also
have heard her uncontrollable and rapturous

response to Court's lovemaking. Oddly, it also had
the effect of bringing to mind Court's own last comment—less than committing, to be sure—making her
feel vulnerable now in the face of her own unstinting
ardour, and in consequence she sat up quickly and
swung her legs to the floor, one hand tightly clutch-
ing the edges of her dress together.

'I think you'd—better go,' she said in throaty, and
not altogether steady, accents. Her breathing still
hadn't returned to normal as yet.

Court's own chest rose and fell deeply as he moved
to sit beside her, his outline only just visible in the
faint light that was altering the room from the veranda where the light from Joel's room next door was
now spilling outwards.

'You're probably right,' he acceded heavily, adding with a touch of irony, 'I'm beginning to
understand why Alick was prepared to make such an
effort to have you employed here.'

'Meaning?' she queried dubiously, her eyes unsuccessfully attempting to pierce the inky shadows in
order to make out his expression.

He shrugged as he rose upright. 'You're damned
hard to ignore!'

Implying that he wanted to ignore her? But why?
Just because he didn't like becoming involved with
his staff? Or because he was more than content with
matters as they were; with him unattached and therefore free to pick and choose from among the station's
female visitors? Eden swallowed anguishedly, her
fingers twining together painfully in her lap at the
thought that he saw her as merely a not altogether
wanted diversion. Not that she had any idea what
that had to do with Alick, but then, right at the

moment that was the least of her concerns.

'And you would prefer it if I resigned,' she deduced flatly at length. He had made it all too abundantly clear that he had been adverse to employing her in the first place, after all.

Court drew in a long breath, but instead of responding directly, countered in weighty tones, 'Do you want to?'

Dear God, she knew she should, but. . . *could* she just walk away from him like that, even with things as they were? 'No.' Her barely audible reply seemed to answer both his and her own question.

'Then since I did agree to employ you, that would appear to settle that, wouldn't it?' he returned shortly, beginning to make for the door.

'I guess so,' Eden allowed sombrely, and threw herself on to her stomach as soon as he left, burying her face in her pillow as hot tears gathered at the corners of her eyes and she succumbed to a bout of weeping that expressed the misery she was feeling, but did little to ease the pain of its cause.

From then on, Eden applied herself to her work with a dedication that was almost fanatical in an attempt to keep herself so busy that there would be no time for extraneous thoughts to enter her mind. It was also for the sake of her pride, to try to convey to Court the impression that those arousing moments in his arms had meant as little to her as they evidently had to him.

For a while she was successful, too, but as the days passed she gradually became aware that her heart wasn't to be denied quite so easily, so that whereas she had been doing everything possible to avoid

Court's company and only barely looking at him when she couldn't, she then discovered herself to be unconsciously awaiting his appearance, her eyes covertly and ungovernably straying in his direction with increasing insistence.

That he, in turn, gave her a wide berth too unless it was absolutely unavoidable, she supposed she should have been thankful for. But contrarily, she wasn't. It just made her long to hear him talk to her in that provoking drawl of his again—precisely as he seemed to be doing more and more with Crystal! A fact that had a shaft of unbearable pain lancing through her every time she saw them together. Just as it did the afternoon Crystal voluntarily spoke to her for the first time since that fateful barbecue a fortnight before.

'I just came to let you know that Valda left this morning,' the dark-haired girl began with an obviously pleased smile as she sauntered into the office where Eden happened to be working.

Eden's forehead creased slightly as she wondered just what was being led up to. 'I know,' she acknowledged. 'The rest of the staff organised something of a send-off party for her in Gaye's quarters last night.' Not that Crystal had deigned to turn up, she recalled, even though she had been invited.

'Well, now there's room in the staff quarters there's no need for you to remain in the homestead, is there?' Crystal proposed with a smirk. 'Court's suggested that *you* should share Dyna's room with her now.'

'I see,' Eden forced out past stiff lips. He couldn't even tell her himself, but had left it to Crystal, of all people, to do so! Pushing back her chair, she rose to her feet, valiantly refusing to let the other girl see how devastated she felt. 'I'll go and start packing my things now, then.'

'It would seem advisable,' Crystal had no compunction in agreeing. She smiled, although it didn't reach her eyes. 'That way you can be all settled in before the rush starts later.'

Plus save herself the embarrassment of having Court return before she had finished, added Eden as she hurried across to the homestead. Once inside, it didn't take her long to pile everything into the two cases she had brought with her and, after ensuring there was no sign in the room to indicate she had ever occupied it, to stow it all in her car and drive down to the staff quarters.

The accommodation she was to share with Dyna was compact, but quite adequate, and similar in design to all those other units occupied by members of the staff. There were two beds, a couch, a table and some chairs, a couple of cupboards, and a kitchenette separated from the rest by a built-in bench. The washing facilities were communal and situated at the end of the block. It wasn't quite on a par with the homestead, of course, Eden mused, but then Dyna's presence wasn't likely to prove as disturbing to have around as someone else's had been either.

'Oh, hi!' Dyna herself suddenly pulled open the screen door and came into the room. 'Crystal just told me you were moving in, so I thought I'd come and see how you were doing,' she smiled. 'Are you usually tidy, or untidy?' Her head tilted enquiringly.

'Usually tidy,' Eden grinned. 'Although I must admit things have been known to become a little out of control on occasion.'

'The same here,' the other girl confessed with a laugh. 'But that's good. We should get along fine.

Valda nearly sent me mad the way she left everything scattered all over the place! Anyway, if everything's okay,' she continued without a break, 'I guess I'd better be getting back to the kitchen. Norma's trying out a new dish for dinner tonight, so at the moment it's all hands to the wheel.' She gave another laugh and turned back for the door.

'Oh, before you go. . .!' Eden called after her hurriedly, continuing once Dyna had halted and swung to face her again, 'Would you know where I could park my car? I can't just leave it out the front, it blocks anyone else from getting through.'

'Why not just put it back where you had it before?' suggested Dyna with a shrug. 'It was under the homestead, wasn't it? There's certainly plenty of room there.'

Eden frowned. 'But now I'm not staying there, I don't think they'd like. . .'

'Oh, I shouldn't think the boss would mind,' Dyna inserted confidently. 'He might give you one of those wry looks of his, but I doubt if he'd actually say anything. As you must know from having stayed in the house.' She smiled eloquently. 'He's really something special, isn't he?'

Although in no mood to agree at the moment, Eden still had no wish to raise suspicions by demurring. In lieu, she merely offered a supposedly concurring, 'Mmm. . .' in reply.

'Anyhow, that's where I'd park it,' advised Dyna, preparing to leave once more.

Eden simply nodded and let her go, then sighed and surmised she had little choice if she didn't want to leave it in the open, where the tropical sun would take the shine and the colour out of the paintwork in no time.

Not that Court's reaction to the situation was anything like Dyna had forecast, though, she discovered, when she happened to meet him on leaving the restaurant after finishing her dinner that evening. She had taken to having it early with Gaye and other minor members of the staff most nights in order to avoid his disruptive company.

There was no wry look for her, she noted half despondently, half bitterly, as he stopped her when she would have continued past him. Nothing so tolerant or lazy, in fact. The glance she received was closer to furious and withering.

'I hear you moved out of the homestead this afternoon,' he said with something of a snap, but still in a low tone because of the numbers present in the bar.

It didn't take much to guess just who hadn't been able to wait to pass on the piece of good news, Eden grimaced sarcastically to herself, and angled her head higher. 'That's right. I thought it preferable to do it as soon as possible.' She paused, her expression becoming a trifle gibing. 'As I also thought you would prefer it too.' Particularly since he hadn't even had the decency to inform her himself!

Court's jaw tightened, and a dark brow arched satirically. 'Although I note you appear to consider it's good enough for your car to remain there!'

She caught at her lip with even white teeth. She *knew* she shouldn't have gone along with Dyna's suggestion. 'I'll move it straight away!' she proposed stiffly, starting to take her leave—until his fingers closed about her arm and brought her to a standstill once again.

'To where?'

'Oh, don't panic, I'll make sure it's nowhere where it might take up any space you may require, or where it might cause you any inconvenience!'

'That isn't what I meant!'

'No?' Eden widened her eyes sceptically, caustically. 'Well, don't worry, I'll find somewhere! I'll ask Jim Stanley. At least *he's* game enough to pass on his own directions!'

'And just what's that suppose to imply?' Court bit out direfully.

'I'm sure you'll be able to work it out if you really put your mind to it!' she quipped with scornful facetiousness. 'After all, with the ability you have for keeping so many facts and figures in your head, it really is a bit much to expect someone to believe you could forget having. . .'

'Hello, stranger, have you come to join us?' Nick suddenly interrupted as he appeared from out of the crowd. 'We've hardly seen you of late—not even during dinner.'

'And that's a circumstance that can change too as from tomorrow!' put in Court on a resolute, uncompromising note. His aquamarine eyes locked with tawny-gold. 'Since the tourists eat at the later time, then so will the Tourist Manager!'

Eden's breasts heaved with indignant, resentful emotion. Just because she had seen fit to chide him for not relaying his own instructions, he now had to demonstrate who always held the upper hand by laying down more laws in retaliation, did he? 'But since I have already eaten *this* evening. . .' She looked pointedly at the hand restraining her even as she began pulling against it, and promptly moved further away when it was withdrawn.

'You mean, you're not going to join us, then?' queried Nick on a disappointed note.

'Sorry. . .' she half smiled regretfully, albeit only for his sake. As it happened, she hadn't spent much time with Nick either since the night of the barbecue. 'I've got a lot to do.' She turned to make her way out of the bar.

'Hell's bells! You must be working her to death, old son!' she heard him charge Court humorously as she left.

'Oh, why don't you shut up, Nick!' was the surprisingly explosive, and definitely unamused return. 'It's Golden Girl's decision, not mine!'

On hearing that particular description once more, and being subjected to the connotations it held for her, Eden was almost tempted to go back and really take him to task about it. But then, in view of the day's events, she wondered wretchedly if it really mattered any more, and continued on her way.

No matter what he believed, by shifting her out of the homestead at the earliest opportunity, hadn't Court as good as told her that he wasn't interested in becoming involved with her any further? If he ever had been!

A state of affairs that had her contemplating, not for the first time, just why she continued putting herself through all the pain and heartache when it would have been so easy to resign. At the same time, the thought of never seeing Court again was something else to consider and, at present, she wasn't too sure she could make that decision with any objectivity. Besides, she reasoned assuringly, she liked her job there. It was interesting; it was certainly set in a picturesque and unusual environment; and she met a lot of very nice people—Des Porter and Crystal Lamont notwithstanding!

Even so, and despite her attempts to immerse herself totally in her work, Eden found it almost impossible to banish Court from her thoughts, especially when her every sense seemed only too aware of him whenever he appeared. And never more so than the evening three days later when she told him that the prints of her photographs had arrived at last.

'I guess you'd better bring then over to the homestead, then, so we can go over them,' Court proposed.

'Oh—but they're only in the office. I thought. . .' Eden demurred with a different but implicit shrug. The homestead conjured up memories she preferred not to resurrect.

A muscle flickered at the side of his jaw. 'Yeah, well, I'm sorry if the house is such a distastful reminder for you,' he retorted pungently, if mistakenly. Her memories were perturbingly evocative rather than distasteful. 'None the less, after having been incarcerated in the office for some hours this afternoon, I've no wish to spend *my* whole evening there as well, so as I said. . . you'd better bring them across to the homestead.'

Eden sighed defeatedly. 'And—er—shall I bring the text too that I've been working on to go with them?

'Since it's a necessary part of any brochure, it would seem logical, don't you think?' sardonically succinct.

She coloured self-consciously and swallowed. 'So what time should I bring them across?'

'Now would appear as good a time as any.' He paused, a dark brow peaking significantly. 'Unless, of course, you have some pressing personal engagement to fulfil first.'

Meaning with Nick? Eden shook her head and answered in as businesslike a manner as she could manage. 'No, now will be quite satisfactory.' If it had to be done at all. 'I—I'll go and collect everything and meet you over there.'

Court gave a short nod, already turning to leave, and expelling another dismal breath, Eden did likewise with somewhat lagging steps. So far his attitude had hardly been conducive to a particularly interested or even impartial viewing and estimation of her work. Nor an especially comfortable evening!

Eventually, armed with all the relevant material, Eden made her way to the homestead and up the stairs, hesitating before the ever-open door momentarily in order to gather about her like a protective shield all the composure she could muster before raising her hand and knocking.

'Oh, for heaven's sake! Since when have you considered it necessary to knock before coming in here?' Court demanded impatiently as he answered the summons and pushed open the flyscreen door.

Eden's brows rose fractionally in surprise. 'Since I moved out, naturally,' she returned coolly as she squeezed past him, although inwardly she felt herself grow warm with an uncontrollable awareness on unavoidably brushing against his muscular frame.

'Ah, yes, just something else to be discontinued, huh?'

She spared him a speculative look over her shoulder as she moved towards the sitting-room, but didn't reply. Not quite certain as to his meaning, although not to his apparent mood which seemed to have changed little since she had spoken to him in the bar, she considered it less likely to prove unsettling if she restricted her comments to her reason for being there.

The fact that Court didn't pursue the matter either made her glad she had kept her silence and enabled her to follow him in a slightly less apprehensive state of mind from the sitting-room into the dining-room where there were some papers already resting on the smoked-glass-topped table.

'Would you like a drink?' Court lifted an enquiring brow as she deposited the padded envelope containing the photographs and her typewritten notes on the table.

Feeling some fortification could be beneficial, Eden nodded. 'Just something long and cool, please.'

'Wine and fruit juice?'

'Thank you,' she accepted, and took the seat opposite the one he had evidently been using while he poured her drink, and retrieved a beer for himself, from the wood-panelled bar in the sitting-room.

'Here.' He handed her the crystal goblet on his return, together with a coaster mat to absorb the inevitable condensation. His own drink he kept in the can, surrounded by a foam holder.

Nodding her acknowledgement, Eden took a sip of the wine, appreciating its cool tingle as it slid refreshingly down her dry throat. Then, placing the long-stemmed glass on the coaster, she began to extract the folders of photographs from the envelope.

'I've sorted them all under different headings. Accommodation, the complex in general, activities, flora and fauna, that sort of thing,' she explained as she handed them across the table. 'I thought it would be easier that way to view them in relation to the appropriate text.'

Court inclined his head slightly, leaning back in his chair and eyeing her expressively from between thickly lashed, half-closed lids. 'You don't also think it would make the whole exercise easier if you sat here,' indicating the seat next to his, 'instead of doing it upside down from over there?'

To be truthful, Eden preferred it the way it was. 'I—well—it's no trouble for me to recognise the photos, and—and I've been working on the text so long that I just about know it by heart,' she parried.

'And if I want something clarified? He crooked an ironic brow. 'It would be far simpler if we could both see everything with equal ease, don't you think?' As he paused, the contours of his shapely mouth edged into a mocking curve. 'You don't have to worry, I'm not suggesting it with any nefarious plan in mind.'

'I didn't suppose you were!' she immediately denied, vexedly, and rose quickly to her feet. If she protested any further, it would only make it appear that was precisely the reason she was reluctant to move. Once she had made her way round the table and taken the seat next to him her own wing-tipped brows arched challengingly. 'Satisfied?'

Court didn't answer. He merely fixed her with an unwavering, speaking glance from above the rim of his can as he took a swallow, so that in the end it was Eden who dropped her gaze to the material on the table.

'Is—is there any particular group you want to look at first?' she rushed to enquire, if a trifle throatily, her fingers fiddling nervously with the folders.

'As they come will do,' he declared on a heavily released breath.

Without looking up, Eden nodded and placed all the folders in front of him, her hands clasping anxiously in her lap as he began to thumb through them slowly, thoroughly, and she tried to concentrate all her attention on the matter at hand. The photos were good, technically, she knew that, the images still with a very high resolution despite their considerable enlargement, the colour rendition good, and with no sign of any film break-up while Clive had done his usual excellent work in their printing.

But would Court *like* them, that was the question. The scenes that appealed to one person didn't necessarily have the same effect on someone else, and knowing the subject as well as he did, he could perhaps even consider there were other views and scenes available on the property that would provide an even better representation. Not that she quite knew how. She was sure she had covered every possible angle. But still, there was always that chance, she had to concede.

It took a while for Court to inspect them all—some for longer periods than others—and by the time he had concluded, Eden was sitting on the edge of her chair. 'Well?' she queried with bated breath almost before he had replaced the very last one in its folder

Court turned to face her slowly, his expression giving nothing away—until a wry sweep caught at the edges of his lips. 'You're certainly a surprise package, aren't you, honey?' he finally let his thoughts be known in a lazy drawl.

'Meaning you like them?' she deduced with a spontaneous smile of relief.

He dipped his head. 'It would be difficult not to. They're great. . . as you must know.'

She hunched a deprecating shoulder. 'Yes, well, I knew were okay technically, but that was no guarantee they would actually appeal to you. I tried to capture the essence of Arrunga River as I saw it—as a visitor here might—and just hoped the concept would find favour in your eyes too,' she explained with an ungovernable bubbling enthusiasm in her pleasure. 'This is also how I envisaged the brochure being laid out,' she went on in the same eager fashion, showing him the mock-up she had already designed. 'I thought about a dozen or so photos would be sufficient, although that, and their selection, is up to you, of course.' She paused briefly. 'I was also wondering if you'd ever given any thought to producing a book, or a coloured booklet, on the station. You know, one detailing the history of the property right from its earliest days, how it came about, the trials and tribulations of its pioneers, the fact that the region as a whole is still very much as it was when the first explorers came through here over a hundred years ago, explaining the stories behind such intriguing names for places as Attack Creek, Skeleton Yard, Disputed Flats, Accident Waterhole, Misery Hill—just to name a few. I've had quite a number of people ask me if there was something available in that line, and Jim Stanley's told me that there's a wealth of stories relating to the property. I'm sure it would make fascinating reading, and—and. . .' She came to an abashed halt, her cheeks colouring warmly, and abruptly aware that she was letting her enthusiasm run away with her. As a result, when she next spoke it was in noticeably discomfited tones. 'And I'm straying from the subject. I'm sorry. Wh-what do you think of the 'ayout?'

'I haven't exactly had time to look at it as yet.' Court's stating of the obvious was delivered on a drily implicit note that had Eden's cheeks staining afresh.

'I'm sorry,' she apologised again in a small voice.

'What for? I've no objection to listening to new ideas. . . and especially when expounded in such a vital and animated manner.'

'Oh!' Eden moistened her lips self-consciously, and wished she hadn't when the unthinking action seemed to act like a magnet for Court's unsettling blue-green gaze. 'You—you might be prepared to consider it, then?'

For a moment or two he didn't reply as his eyes remained fixed on the soft curves of her mobile mouth, and then he gave a sharp shake of his head, scrubbed a hand through his hair, and turned back to the papers on the table. 'Perhaps,' he allowed brusquely.

Eden bit her lip and reached for her wine in order to take a couple of calming mouthfuls. His nearness, his glance, his every inflection, seemed capable of disturbing her, but she tried desperately not to let it show as she extracted a typewritten sheet from among the rest and placed it beside the mock-up he was surveying. 'That's the text for each of the blank sections,' she advised as evenly as possible.

Court simply nodded and switched his attention to the first of the paragraphs on the sheet, while almost against her will, Eden found her gaze being drawn to his clear-cut profile as he read. His now tousled hair fell on to his forehead slightly, lending a boyish look to what was indisputably a man's face, his surprisingly long lashes throwing shadows on to his sun-darkened cheeks, the corners of his sensuous mouth still quirking upwards even when tautly set.

He looked startlingly handsome, and Eden felt her heart contract as she stared at him, a deep feeling of longing suddenly assaulting her senses. Then, as if the strength of her emotions had somehow managed to communicate itself to him, Court abruptly glanced in her direction, his eyes locking with hers inexorably

All at once the atmosphere seemed electrically charged, the tension in the air almost palpable, and Eden's throat worked convulsively. 'I'm—I—do you. . .' she began, moving her hands flusteredly and, because she had forgotten the glass she was still holding, bumping against the table and spilling its remaining contents across the smooth surface. Dragging her gaze from his at last, she flushed and got hastily to her feet, feeling even more self-conscious as she deposited the now empty glass on its coaster. 'I'm sorry. I—I'll get something to wipe it up.'

'Don't bother! I'll do it,' rasped Court, pushing himself upright.

'It's no. . .' She halted abruptly as they collided on both turning for the kitchen, and looked up compulsively on sensing him stiffen.

With a low groan of frustration, he jerked her into his arms, a hand tangling in her hair and holding her head motionless as his mouth took hers in a hard and burning demand. His lips were insistent, relentless, depriving her of the will and the wish to do anything but respond, and shocking her with the force of her own abandoned feelings.

Every taut line of his muscled body was pressed urgently to hers, and she clung to him helplessly, boneless and melting. She wanted him. Wanted him as she had never wanted any man before. Wanted to experience again the arousing feel his bare skin against hers as she had once before, and wanted his complete possession of her in the most fulfilling way possible.

Then Court's fingers, still entwined within her hair, suddenly drew her head back, and he set his warm mouth roughly to the fragile arch of her slender throat. 'You sure know how to play havoc with a man's senses, don't you, honey?' he growled on a strangely harsh note.

Fighting to regain some control over her emotions, Eden stared at him dazedly, her breathing shallow and ragged. He made it sound as if she was—practised—at such things, and the thought had her face burning as much with resentment as humiliation. 'Then maybe *you* shouldn't have kissed me!' she choked in defence, pulling away from him.

'I'll go along with that!' he seemed more than willing to concede, and a knot of welling despair lodged in her throat as he turned away.

'I'll clean up the mess,' she just managed to push out unsteadily, waving a hand vaguely towards the spilt wine.

'Leave it!' Court's veto was accompanied by a terse shake of his head. He paused, inhaling deeply. 'And it might be best if we forgot about these too,' indicating the photographs cursorily.

Eden swallowed painfully. 'You're not interested in them any more?'

'Right at the moment, no!' He uttered a sharp, mocking laugh. 'Or did you really think either of us could continue as if nothing had happened?'

She averted her gaze discomfitedly, and it chanced upon the liquid still lying on the table, causing her to shift from one foot to the other indecisively. 'Are you sure I can't. . .'

'Oh, for God's sake, just get out of here, will you, Eden!' Count interjected savagely, his eyes holding a hard challenge as they connected with hers.

She pressed her lips together to conceal their sudden trembling. So once again she was being turned out of the homestead. 'I'm sorry,' she whispered brokenly, although she had no idea just what she was apologising for, and took to her heels before the anguished tears that had begun to sting her eyes could spill on to her lashes.

CHAPTER EIGHT

By the following morning Eden's heart still felt as heavy as it had the night before, her feelings as ambivalent, her thoughts as dejected. Although she didn't realise any were outwardly visible until Joel happened to drive past. At the time she was deep in thought and sitting on the creek bank near the landing stage after having just checked that all the boats' fuel tanks were full and ready for the day's hire, when he came by in one of the property's Land Rovers. However, instead of continuing on his way when she lifted a hand in acknowledgement of his wave, to her surprise he stopped to alight and headed down the bank also.

'Is something wrong?' she looked up to ask curiously, albeit in rather flat tones.

A corner of his mouth crooked wryly as he sank down on his haunches beside her. 'Judging by your—shall we say, uncustomarily lacklustre?—wave just now, I thought *you* might consider there was.'

Eden frowned. 'I don't understand.'

He hunched a denim-clad shoulder, half smiling at her askance. 'You've had another run-in with Court, haven't you?'

Was it so obvious? She forced a smile of feigned unconcern to her lips and shrugged. 'So why should that upset me? We have those all the time. . . or haven't you noticed?' A touch of irony entered her voice.

'I meant. . . of a personal kind,' Joel elucidated drily.

Eden bent her head, even white teeth worrying at a soft lower lip. He couldn't possibly have guessed that from her demeanour, could he? Or had Court been so generous as to tell him? She drew a long breath, still avoiding looking at him, and temporised, '*Another* run-in with him?'

'Mmm,' he confirmed. 'My room was next to yours in the homestead, remember?' Pausing slightly, he looked down at the ground and then back at her again. 'I could hear you crying that night I—er—offered to turn off the lights.'

'Oh!' Eden couldn't control the wave of colour that surged into her cheeks. 'I—I'm sorry if I disturbed you.'

Joel shook his head with uncharacteristic impatience. 'Don't be stupid! I was explaining, not complaining. . . as you very well know.' He swept off his hat and ran his fingers through his dark blond hair. 'If it makes you feel any better, Court hasn't escaped entirely unscathed either. He was like a bear with a sore head when I returned to the homestead last night, and. . .' his lips twisted eloquently, 'nor was there much of an improvement this morning. All of which, I might add, is most unusual for Court.'

'Yes, well, when he finally condescends to divulge just what *is* bugging him, then we'll all know what's going on, won't we?' she retorted tartly, grimacing.

'And is that all it means to you?'

Eden caught her breath. Just what was he asking? How much Court really meant to her? Her initial inclination was to disguise her feelings, but then she wondered what would be the point when he obviously already realised she wasn't exactly indifferent to his half-brother, anyway. Picking up a stone, she tossed it disconsolately into the creek.

'No, it means a whole lot more to me than that,' she admitted quietly with a sigh. There was a brief hesitation, and she added with an ungovernable catch in her voice, 'I just wish I knew why he apparently dislikes the idea so much of—of becoming involved with me, that's all.'

Joel looked at her strangely. 'You can't guess?'

Momentarily, her brows flew high in surprise, then lowered to a frown. 'How do you mean?'

He studied her for a second or two before replying. Then, when he did, it wasn't quite the answer she had expected. 'Let's just say. . . I suspect his head is resisting relinquishing control of his thinking,' he relayed ruefully.

'But—but why?' She stared at him in bewilderment.

'Oh, come off it, Eden!' he urged promptly, to her astonishment, and cast her a highly graphic sideways glance. 'You can't be *that* obtuse!'

'Well, evidently I am!' she flared on a somewhat huffy note, becoming tired of people presuming she possessed some knowledge she just didn't have.

He exhaled deeply, looking uncertain whether to believe her or not. 'Then not to put too fine a point on it. . . I once again suspect he's finding it damned difficult to accept that he's not exactly uninterested in picking up where Alick left off!' Shrugging, he continued almost immediately, 'Not that you can really blame him either, I guess. After all, no matter how well he and Alick have always got along together, or how much he tried to put it out of his mind, I reckon it would still be awful hard to take, and even harder not to remember every time Alick puts in an appearance, the knowledge that you and he had been lovers first.'

Momentarily, Eden could only stare at him in stunned disbelief, and then she erupted furiously. 'Except that Alick and I never *have* been lovers!' she blazed. 'I've never even been out with him, in fact! God! As engaging a bloke as Alick is, I've known him for too long, and seen him in operation too often, to ever even contemplate being just another in the long, long line of his live-in companions!' She dragged in a deep breath, a hint of confusion suddenly making an appearance in the depths of her stormy eyes. 'And—and why in heaven's name would anyone think I had been, anyway?'

Looking somewhat surprised himself now, Joel hunched a broad shoulder, but in something of a discomfited manner on this occasion. 'I—well—since it's been his custom in the past, we naturally all just thought. . .'

'What's been his custom in the past?' she broke in to demand.

'To use Arrunga River as a dumping ground for his ex-lovers once his interest begins to—er—wane.'

'He does *what*?' Eden exclaimed, aghast.

'Sends his girl-friends here when he wants to break off his affair with them,' Joel repeated in ironic tones. 'I gather it's his way of doing it gently. . . or conveniently. Of course whether they see it that way, I wouldn't know, because when he arranges for them to come out here they all seem to be under the impression that he'll be joining them in a day or so. . . only he never does!' His mouth shaped crookedly. 'In the meantime, though, his deserted little charmers usually start casting interested eyes in Court's direction, forgetting all about the guy they're supposedly waiting for—just as Alick planned they should, I suspect—and pursue him for all they're worth instead.'

Despair, and a simmering agitation, washed over Eden in towering waves. Oh, God, and everyone had apparently believed she was here to do the same! Now she could understand so many things! And to think Alick had suggested that she should hassle Court, *follow him even*. . . in much the same manner as all his girl-friends evidently had! she supposed irately. Oh, she would kill him the next time she saw him for having created such an intolerable situation!

'But—but surely the fact that, unlike the others, he came *with* me. . .' she tried to reason at length.

'Mmm, that certainly made you different, I admit, but. . .'

'But only so far as you all thought it meant I was simply being rewarded for some special reason, is that what you're trying to say?' she cut in tartly as she abruptly recalled a remark Court had made in the office on her first night there.

'Something like that, I guess,' Joel owned wryly.

'How very considerate of everyone!' she gibed. Her gaze turned reproachful. 'I thought you, at least, were a friend.'

'Would I have stopped today to see if there was anything I could do to help, if I wasn't?' he countered gently. 'And I can assure you that, no matter what anyone believes, you've still made a good many friends among the staff too.'

She had believed so. However. . . 'That evidently still doesn't appear to have convinced anyone I don't sleep around, though, does it?' She pulled a sardonic face. 'Not even you. In fact, for all I know, you may not even believe me *now*.' She bit at her lip, her expression turning anxious. 'But it's the truth, Joel! Alick and I haven't ever been anything more than acquaintances! Give me credit for being a little more intelligent than to add my name to his list of numerous lovers, please!'

Joel nodded reassuringly. 'You want me to prove I believe you by convincing Court for you?' he grinned.

She shook her head decisively. 'No! I don't want anyone convincing Court of anything on my behalf! Thank you all the same,' she added with a softening half-smile, and in considerably less fierce tones. 'Besides, I'm not even sure if I care any more.'

His lips twitched. 'Now why do I get the feeling you don't really mean that?'

Eden pulled irritably at some blades of grass. 'Well, I should,' she sniffed. Her lashes suddenly felt damp and she rubbed the back of her hand swiftly across them. 'Oh, damn him! Why *should* I have to explain myself?' She gave a rejecting shake of her head. 'And nor will I! Maybe I'll just give him some of his own back instead!'

Joel sucked in an expressive whistling breath between his teeth and laughed. 'Now this I have just got to see!'

'Why? Don't you think I'm capable of doing so?'

'I wouldn't doubt it for one minute.' He smiled broadly. 'It's the fireworks that are likely to ensue that I'm interested in watching.'

'Because he won't appreciate someone sitting in judgment on him for a change?' she sniped.

'More like, he could consider it a challenge.'

'To his authority?'

Joel grinned wryly. 'As to that, I guess it's for you to discover. Just make certain you don't bite off more than you can chew, hmm?' He tapped her lightly beneath the chin in emphasis.

Something that was a distinct possibility, Eden had to concede. It was all very well planning to haul Court over the coals, but exactly how she was to do so she wasn't quite sure as yet. Moreover, even if she did succeed in correcting his mistaken assumption that she was just another of Alick's girls, just where did she go from there? And how? When all was said and done, there was still no guarantee that his emotions were involved to the same extent hers were! Which depressing thought remained in the forefront of her mind long after Joel had finally continued on his way and she had returned to the complex.

Shortly after lunch, however, an event occurred that added even another dimension to her problems. Out of the blue, Simone and Wade Seaton arrived home in a chartered plane piloted by none other than Alick! Their appearance, so totally unexpected, created considerable excitement for a time as the word rapidly passed round and they were enthusiastically and eagerly welcomed home by all the staff present.

One of the first to do so was Crystal, who, as anxious as she obviously was to hurry across to the homestead, still delayed long enough as she passed the counter where Eden was working to favour her with a satisfied smile and some unsolicited advice.

'Of course, now that Simone and Wade are home, you may as well start packing straight away, because you're now completely superfluous!' she positively gloated. 'They've always managed all the tourist activities previously, and they certainly won't be requiring any help from you!'

'Not even until they've settled in again?' countered Eden with protective mockery, refusing to show just how dismayed she was by the arrival of Court's mother and stepfather. She had already realised that it put her position in doubt.

'Well, maybe for a couple of days,' Crystal was prepared to concede airily. 'I just wanted to ensure you understood the position. After all, you were never needed or wanted here. . . as anyone with the slightest degree of sensitivity would have acknowledged, and therefore departed, long ago! Much to his regret, Court only agreed to hire you as a favour to Alick, and you've been an embarrassment to everyone ever since. Although not for much longer, thank goodness!' With another exultant smile she took her departure.

Eden was grateful to see her leave, although not for the opportunity it provided to ponder over what the other girl had said. Did Court regret having employed her, and to such an extent that he had discussed the matter with Crystal? Were her days at Arrunga River now numbered?

The latter had been her own immediate thought on learning of Simone and Wade's return, but although she had half attempted to view the prospect with relief—it would solve all her problems, bar one, after all—it was that one, that single most important problem, that eventually had her admitting she was only fooling herself by pretending she would be anything but desolated on leaving the property—and its undeniably stirring owner!

Sighing, and unable to concentrate properly any more, Eden closed the book she had been working on and moved out from behind the counter, preparing to go down to one of the stores sheds to check that everything was in readiness for the camp-out trail ride that was due to get under way the next morning.

She was about to tell Gaye, filling in at the bar during Crystal's absence, where she might be found should anyone need her services, when a familiar male figure entered the area and immediately crossed towards them.

'Well, and how are my two favourite girls?' Alick smiled disarmingly on coming to a halt beside Eden.

'Favourite here, that is,' qualified Gaye with a bantering grin.

Alick tut-tutted in pseudo-reproachful tones. 'Is that all the welcome I get after flying all the way out here?'

'Oh, no!' Eden interposed in silky tones. 'I have much more than that lined up for you, believe me!'

He eyed her aslant, unsure whether she was joking or not. 'Yes, well, I thought I'd come and say, "G'day," since neither of you have been over to the homestead as yet.'

'That's because not *all* of us can drop whatever we're doing as the whim takes us,' put in Gaye expressively.

'Ah, yes, sweet Crystal.' He was quick to pick up the inference. 'I saw her making for the house flat chat in the probable hope of ingratiating herself somehow. It made me more than glad I'd already left.' Pausing, he turned to Eden with another mock-sorrowful expression. 'I did think you might come and bid me hello, though.' Before she could answer, he bent to take a swift look at the now slightly worse for wear badge she had pinned to her T-shirt and exclaimed, 'Good lord! Is that the best identification Court could supply?'

Eden uttered a highly sardonic laugh. 'Don't knock it! I'm lucky to have one at all!' She angled him a dulcetly threatening gaze. 'And one of the reasons I didn't go looking for you at the homestead is because I doubted your father and stepmother would appreciate having blood all over their floor after I'd got through with you!'

'Eh?' Alick blinked, taken aback. 'What have I done?'

'Enough to make me feel like slaughtering you, believe me! And if Gaye will excuse us. . .' with an apologetic look in that girl's direction as she began urging him outside again, 'I'd like nothing better than to—er—discuss it with you right now!'

'Well, I can't honestly imagine what you could possibly be so worked up about,' he declared, shrugging, as they seated themselves at one of the vacant, umbrella-shaded tables surrounding the swimming pool. 'Battered badge or not, you've obviously managed to demonstrate that you're capable of fulfilling the position. . . just as I said would happen.'

'Although not because any thanks were due to you!' Eden promptly charged on a caustic note. She sucked in a deep breath. 'For heaven's sake, Alick, you might at least have had the decency to warn me that you dump your old girl-friends by sending them to Arrunga River!'

'Oh, so you found out about that, did you?' He had the grace to at least look a little abashed. 'Well, it seems a more pleasant way of ending a relationship, although I must admit I can't quite see why that should have made any difference where you're concerned.'

'Because everyone thought *I* was just another of your cast-offs! A belief that wasn't likely to be overcome by my following your suggestions to hassle and chase after Court in order to achieve my purpose. . . just as all your other past conquests damned well do, apparently!'

'But for differing reasons,' Alick defended.

'Not that anyone seems to have noticed!' retorted Eden, grimacing.

'Well, never mind,' he consoled with an imperturbable smile. 'Since you have evidently taken over as Tourist Manager, there's obviously been no harm done.'

No harm done! 'Except that Court, for one, apparently still happens to be of the opinion that I was one of those girls of yours!' she rounded on him heatedly. Her eyes sought his perplexedly. 'Surely you must have told him *something* to the contrary when you persuaded him to hire me that first night we arrived.'

'I—well. . .' He glanced away momentarily. 'I may have done. I can't quite remember.' And with a causal hunching of one shoulder, 'Anyway, does it really matter what he believes, as long as you've got the job?'

Eden stared at him incredulously. 'Yes, of course it does! The more so since I. . .' Her teeth clamped together with an almost audible snap before she could say any more. Before her heightened emotions had her divulging far more than she intended or wanted.

She took a steadying breath and concluded tartly, 'Since *I* don't happen to relish a reputation for indulging in casual affairs!'

'Unlike me, is that what you're getting at?' His lips tilted wryly.

She shook her head helplessly, her own mouth beginning to curve with grudging humour. He was so even-tempered, so unfailingly nonchalant, that it was impossible to remain annoyed with him for any length of time. 'You really are a louse, Alick!' she charged with a rueful half-smile.

He grinned. 'But an agreeable one,' he wasn't above qualifying.

'Unfortunately!' Her accompanying laugh was equally expressively voiced.

'Yes—well—now having got that out of the way. . .' He reached across the table to clasp one of her hands in a friendly gesture. 'Tell me how you've been getting on.'

Eden's features sobered a little and she hunched an evasive shoulder. 'Oh, I've had my ups and downs, failures and successes,' she relayed on a dry note, wanting to avoid revealing too much. 'Nevertheless, now that your father and stepmother have returned. . .' She shrugged, and almost guiltily snatched her hand from his as she suddenly saw Court and Joel nearing the table. She supposed Crystal must have contacted them through the CB for them to have arrived back so early. 'Er—we, or you at any rate, are about to have company,' she advised Alick, who had his back to them, and then promptly responded to the fulminating look on Court's taut-set face with a challenging lift of her head and wished she had left her hand where it was. He could believe what he liked! she decided rebelliously. Why *should* she explain her actions, or feel guilty either, if it came to that?

Not that any such explosive look was evident when he greeted Alick, though, she noted furiously as the older man rose to his feet with obvious pleasure on turning and recognising the other two. Oh, no, it was quite acceptable for Alick to supposedly have an affair with her! She just wasn't supposed to have had one with *him*! she seethed.

'Have you seen Simone and Wade yet?' Alick went on to ask.

Court shook his head. 'Not yet. We were just on our way over there when we saw you.' He flicked a cynically corrosive glance in Eden's direction. 'Talking over old times, hmm?'

'Something like that,' she allowed with a purposely evocative smile, and had the pleasure of seeing his ja   clench tightly.

'I'm sure you must have found it very. . . pleasurable.' His gibe surfaced with a definite bite.

'Oh, yes,' she had no compunction in agreeing sweetly. 'I've always found *Alick's* company most enjoyable,' she added with deliberate emphasis. Although this time her satisfaction at gaining an immediate response was tempered with a little trepidation as his eyes promptly glinted in a manner that boded no good for her at a later date.

'Oh, by the way. . .' Alick broke in, claiming his stepbrother's attention once more, 'I thought I'd better mention it, just in case, but it's been decided that we'll have dinner at the homestead tonight instead of the restaurant. A sort of homecoming celebration, as it were, with all the family included as well as some of the more senior members of the staff.'

Court nodded and slanted Eden a narrowed, mocking gaze. 'That includes you, Golden Girl.'

'Oh, but. . .' she immediately began to demur, judging it considerably more prudent to avoid his presence for a while as a result of that last ominous look, as well as taking exception to his use of that particularly aggravating appellation. 'You said yourself, the Tourist Manager should eat with the visitors.'

For a moment she didn't think he meant to insist as he signalled to Joel that they should continue on their way to the homestead, but when, on passing her chair, he suddenly lowered his head to within unnerving inches of hers, she realised her mistake.

'Be there!' he ordered on such a hard, implacable note that she gulped involuntarily. Drawing back a space, his lips shaped goadingly, and his voice held a softer though no less disturbing danger, he warned, 'Because I wouldn't advise you to put me to the trouble of ensuring that you do attend.'

The threat had Eden pressing her lips together and her amber eyes clashing mutinously with his even as resentment and discretion warred within her, but eventually—she suspected inevitably—discretion won and dropping her gaze she conceded in a throaty murmur, 'I'll be there.'

Court merely gave a curt nod and moved on, leaving Joel to counsel with rueful eloquence as he too passed her chair, 'You're playing with fire, sweetheart! I'd keep my bites just a little smaller, if I were you.'

Eden pulled a partly disgruntled, partly defeated face but didn't reply as he too took his leave, and discovered Alick to be regarding her curiously on having resumed his seat.

'Well, well! And might I be permitted to ask just what that was all about?' he enquired, not altogether straight-faced.

She shrugged. 'I told you I had my ups and downs,' she quipped, trying to make light of it.

'Mmm, you also said you objected to Court believing you and I had had an affair, yet the minute he appears you seem to do your damnedest to give credence to the idea!' he retorted. 'And what in God's name was Joel going on about with his "smaller bites", or whatever?'

'That was just an in-joke,' Eden contended uneasily.

'Oh?' He looked totally disbelieving. 'And the other?'

She shifted restlessly on her seat. 'I—er—let's just say I decided to—to really give him a reason to be annoyed for a change!' she finished in a defiant rush.

'Well, I've got to admit it appears to have worked admirably,' granted Alick drily. 'At a guess, I'd say that with very little extra effort on your part, you could manage to rile him into really exploding.' A graphic twist caught at his lips. 'Of course, whether you'd like the result if you succeeded could be something else again.'

Eden surmised it might be too, but still felt entitled to defend, 'Well, why should I be made to feel in the wrong? It's his fault for not checking his facts! Why couldn't he just take me on t-trust, the same as he—does everyone else here?' Her voice started to break and she averted her gaze, mortified to find her eyes suddenly awash, and desperately trying to hide it.

But not swiftly enough, apparently, for Alick abruptly sat forward, his face losing its humorous expression. 'Oh boy! I think I'm beginning to see the light. There's a whole lot more to this than you've mentioned to date, isn't there, sweetie?'

'I don't know what you're talking about,' she denied in husky accents.

He wouldn't allow her to sidestep the issue that easily, however. 'I'm talking about the fact that you happen to have fallen heavily for my stepbrother!' Halting, he ran a hand distractedly through his hair. 'God! That was one eventuality I didn't anticipate!'

If she wasn't more careful soon everyone would know how she felt about Court! Eden despaired, although astonishment at Alick's latter words had her temporarily forgetting her dismay. 'Meaning?' she queried with a frown.

'What?' He stared at her blankly as if having been lost in thought, and then gave a quick half-laugh. 'Oh, pay no attention to me, I was merely thinking aloud.' And returning to his original line of questioning, 'I'm right in what I said, though, aren't I?'

She sighed, and nodded. With her eyes still misty and her lashes wet, it seemed a little too much to expect him to believe otherwise.

'Then why on earth haven't you attempted to explain just how things really stand between us?' He hesitated. 'Or have you?'

'No!' Her mouth set resolutely. 'I have my pride too, you know! Besides, what am I supposed to say? That I'd appreciate it if he would change his mind about me because I happen to be in love with him and would very much like him to feel the same way about me? I don't know if he would, even if I did manage to convince him,' she choked.

'Oh, hell! I'm sorry.' A pained look crossed Alick's face. 'It seems *I'd* better have a word with him, doesn't it?'

'Don't you dare!' gasped Eden, surprising him. 'If he can't—if he's not prepared—if he doesn't. . .' She halted, conscious that she wasn't making sense, and scrambled to her feet. 'I'm sorry. I'd rather not talk about it any more, if you don't mind. And—and as people are starting to return. . .' a hasty look round had shown that, 'I'll see you at dinner.' She spun on her heel and began hurrying away, hoping against hope that no one would stop to speak to her before she reached her quarters.

As it was, she managed to make it to the corner of the building without sighting anyone, but on turning it found the person she least wanted to see right then striding towards her from the opposite direction. Just why Court wasn't at the homestead as she had imagined, she had no idea, but that wasn't the greatest of her problems. Attempting to recover some of her shattered composure was. That she had also been crying was impossible to camouflage, it appeared judging by his harshly mocking comment as he stepped into her path to bar her progress.

'What's up? Alick given you another rebuff?'

Eden swallowed anguishedly, and it took every ounce of willpower she possessed to keep her head high. 'Why should you care whether he did or not?' she threw back at him acrimoniously.

'Who said I did?' he retorted on a savagely grated note.

Shaking, she dropped her gaze. 'No, I—I should have known better, shouldn't I?' she murmured tremulously, and before he could move to stop her, darted around him and fled into her room just two doors down, thankful beyond belief that Dyna was away visiting her parents in Mount Isa for a couple of days.

Briefly, it seemed Court meant to follow her, but then he gave a dismissive shake of his head, his mouth setting into hard-edged lines, and he continued on his way determinedly.

Dinner at the homestead that evening was a harrowing experience for Eden despite the kindly efforts of Simone and Wade—as she also was invited to call them—to put her at her ease since it was apparent, and seemingly uncontrollably so, to Eden's dismay, that she was as nervous as a cat on hot bricks. Although not for the reason of meeting Simone and Wade and joining the family for the meal, as she surmised everyone probably supposed.

It was purely due to Court's disruptive presence and his, if not openly antagonistic as it had been earlier, then at least sardonically goading attitude, which was brought into play right from the moment she arrived. It had been he who had taken it upon himself to introduce her to his mother and stepfather, and his mother's smiling assessment of their newest staff member evidently hadn't found favour with him.

'Oh, what a pretty girl!' Simone had exclaimed impulsively, holding out a welcoming hand as they neared her.

'Yeah, pretty damned impossible!' Court had promptly charged in a long-suffering drawl that had the light, self-conscious flush that had suffused Eden's cheeks at his parent's remark deepening even further.

'Oh, I can't believe that,' Simone had denied with a smile, her eyes, much the same colour as her son's, twinkling. 'And especially not when I've been hearing just how well Eden's been doing.'

'Mmm, she's quite made us unnecessary, by the sound it,' Wade had put in with a laugh.

'Although not now you're home again, of course!' Court had been swift to counter, and Eden had felt herself freeze inside. It was more or less what she had been expecting, but that he should sound so thankful at the prospect was almost unbearable.

'I don't know about that,' Wade had then contradicted, exchanging a humorously knowing glance with his wife. 'As a matter of fact, we thought we might only remain at home for a month or two before setting off again. We've still a lot of friends, and places, to see yet, and we're not getting any younger.'

'Positively ancient, in fact!' Court had declared, eyeing the pair of them—in their middle fifties, and obviously extremely healthy—drily.

'Yes, well, not that any of that's either here nor there at the moment,' Simone had broken in to contend, and proceeded to give Eden a charming smile. 'You still haven't actually introduced us as yet.'

Once those formalities had been completed, Eden took her leave of the three of them as soon as she politely could. Grateful to Crystal for the first time ever when it was that girl joining them and proceeding to take over the conversation that provided the opportunity.

After that, she had done her best to evade Court's company altogether, and thus his scarcely veiled and often unsettling remarks, but simultaneously he had seemed equally determined that she shouldn't escape for long for, no matter who she spoke to or where she moved to, he would eventually put in an appearance too. Whether he did so because of her presumed relationship with Alick, or whether she herself had caused it by her own provoking comments that afternoon, Eden didn't know. She only knew that her every sense and emotion was becoming increasingly lacerated and ragged as the evening progressed.

Her only respite was during the meal itself when, to her heartfelt relief, she found herself seated between Joel and Jim Stanley, the latter neatly spruced up and even shaved for the occasion, which was something he did only rarely. Although even then she wasn't allowed to get away completely scot free.

As it happened, it was Simone who inadvertently brought her brief period of peace to an end, and probably only then in a mistakenly genial effort to draw Eden into some conversation since she had refrained from entering any prior ones.

'Court tells me it was you, Eden, who took those beautiful photographs of the property that I saw in the study,' she began in genuinely appreciative tones. 'You must have put a great deal of time and effort into them.'

'*And* a great deal of man-hours, apparently!' Court's immediate insertion was sardonically explicit.

'None of the men had any complaints, did they, Eden?' joked Bryan from the other end of the table.

Again, before she could answer, someone else had another comment to add.

'Why would they?' Crystal half laughed scornfully. 'After all, most of them are on such—close—terms with her.'

'If they are, it's only because they can recognise, and appreciate, quality when they see it!' defended Jim with a growl, to everyone's surprise, and had both girls colouring as a result.

In the sudden silence that followed, Eden turned swiftly, diffidently, to Simone in a desperate attempt to relieve the building tension. 'I—I'm glad you liked them,' she said quietly. 'I've never done anything in a similar vein before.'

Simone smiled. 'Then you've certainly done very well.'

'You see! I told you it was a case of two for the price of one.' Alick cast his stepbrother a triumphant glance.

Court merely returned his gaze steadily.

'And no matter even if some of the men did lend Eden a hand, they still couldn't possibly have lost as much time as we all did when that last photographer was here,' contended Joel, grimacing. 'He had us shifting cattle around for days in order to get the right shots, and even then they didn't turn out to be any good.'

'Probably because he was as nervous as hell immediately any of the cattle came to within a hundred yards of him, if you recall,' laughed Wade.

The memory had the rest of them at the table smiling, even Court, Eden was pleased to note, and the earlier tense moment gradually passed, allowing her to relax at least a little once more.

None the less, as soon as the meal was concluded and they retired to the sitting-room for coffee, she was constantly aware of Court's measuring gaze scrutinising her every move. It promptly destroyed what little equilibrium she had managed to regain, wondering just what he might say or do next, so that when Jim and Bryan eventually prepared to take their leave, she heaved a sigh of relief and immediately followed their example.

She hadn't even reached the stairs leading down from the veranda when she caught the sound of footsteps behind her, some sixth sense telling her who was making them, and she quickened her pace agitatedly.

'Just where do you think you're going?' Court demanded tightly, catching hold of her wrist to bring her to a halt.

Resentment flared as a result of his treatment all evening. 'To my room. . . where I would rather be!'

His mouth curved derisively. 'That's right, you do have a habit of departing the homestead without warning, don't you?'

Eden gasped. He dared to criticise *her* for that? 'I thought you'd prefer it that way. . . since you evidently didn't have the guts to tell me to leave personally!' she jeered.

The fingers about her wrist tightened their grip perceptibly. 'What in hell are you talking about? It was *your* idea to leave like some craven thief in the night!' he grated disparagingly.

'That's a lie! Crystal told me herself that it was your suggestion that I move into the staff quarters!'

'Crystal!' Court's brows snapped together in a frown. 'She told me it was at *your* request!'

It only took a moment for the realisation to dawn on them both as to just what had occurred, and Court glanced back towards the sitting-room where the older girl was still happily ensconced, and muttered something highly graphic under his breath.

'She's gone just too far this time!' he added direfully on a rasping note.

For Eden's part, Crystal's machinations were of little import when compared to her other problems. 'Oh, well, it doesn't matter now, anyway,' she declared wearily, and taking advantage of his diverted attention, broke free of his grasp and started rapidly down the steps.

'And I haven't finished with you yet!' Court advised tersely, following her to the ground.

Despite wheeling to face him, she still continued moving, but backwards. 'You mean there's more?' she gibed, but in a shakier voice than she would have liked.

'Yes, there's more!' he endorsed, keeping pace with her.

Eden felt as if she was being stalked and all her previous nervous tension flooded back. 'Well, *I've* finished with you, and—and I just wish you'd leave me alone!' she cried with a catch in her voice and, turning, broke into a stumbling run.

The shoes she was wearing impeded her progress across the soft grass, however, the high heels sinking deeply into the soil so that she needed all her concentration just to keep from either losing a shoe or twisting an ankle. In consequence, she couldn't really see where she was going—until she walked straight into the path of one of the heavy-duty sprinklers, just as she had on her first day. It was just the last straw as far as Eden was concerned, and she simply stood there momentarily, feeling a complete fool, and burst into uncontrollable tears as the water cascaded over her.

When she did finally move from under the spray it was to find Court waiting for her impassively with his hands resting on his hips, and she burned with humiliation and annoyance. 'Go away!' she ordered distractedly. 'What are you trying to do to me?'

'Probably the same as you've been doing to me ever since you came here!' he retorted roughly, and grasping her by the arm this time, began hustling her along beside him.

Eden shook her head in confusion. And just was that supposed to mean? Trying to break free proved impossible, and in lieu she had to be content with attempting to inject a bolstering firmness into her voice as she demanded anxiously, 'Where are we going?'

'To your room. . . where you said you would rather be!' A group of people came out from the bar as they passed the building and showed an inclination to stop and talk, but Court merely gave them a brief salute and kept walking. 'It seems about the only damned place round here where we're likely to get any privacy!' he ground out irritably.

Being alone with him was the last thing Eden wanted. She was apprehensive of him, and his likely reactions, but most of all she was fearful of her own reactions to *him*. He affected her thoughts and emotions with an ease she seemed to have no way of combating. As a result, she put forward hinderingly, 'Dyna. . .'

'Is in Mount Isa!' He flicked her an expressive glance that told her he was wide awake to her ruse, and proved he was as aware of his staff's whereabouts as she was.

Arriving at the unit, Eden hung back, making a last frantic effort to pull out of his grip as Court opened the door and switched on the light, but to no avail. She was inexorably hauled inside anyway before being released, and the door shut again decisively behind them. In the small area his physical presence was so dominant, so aggressively masculine, that he seemed to fill the whole room, and made her heart start to pound to a flustered, uneasy rhythm, and her tawny eyes to widen as he moved towards her.

'Don't you d-dare touch me!' She said the first thing that came into her mind in her agitation.

'Somebody sure needs to—you're dripping wet,' Court mocked satirically and, dragging a towel from the rail on the wall, had tossed it over her head and proceeded to roughly rub her hair dry himself before she had time to register his intentions.

Embarrassed by what her own unthinking words had implied, Eden immediately turned her vexation on him. 'I can do it myself!' she snapped, putting up a hand to snatch the towel from his grasp. Her fingers only came in contact with stronger hands that determinedly refused to let go, and so she was forced to suffer his ministrations in frustrated silence.

'There! That wasn't too painful, was it?' he taunted when at last he returned the towel to the rail. 'Now I suggest you change into something drier too. What you're wearing has become somewhat distracting. . . not to say distinctly enticing.' He eyed her dress meaningfully.

Looking down, Eden saw that the pink voile that provided a quite adequate covering when dry was now clinging to her like a second skin, outlining her full breasts and her hardened nipples as they pushed against the damp material.

'Oh!' She flushed hotly as she tried to pull the thin cotton away from her body. 'I—well—I can't change while you're here!'

'Oh, for God's sake!' Court erupted impatiently. 'I've already seen you naked to the waist, so what difference does it make?'

New wave of colour surged into her face at the memory. 'It makes a lot of difference because I don't happen to be accustomed to undressing in front of—of. . .'

'Men?' he interrupted harshly. His mouth took on a cynical upturn that she found hateful. 'Why, do you and Alick find it more erotic in the dark?'

Eden gasped in disbelief, then anger bubbled up. 'You bastard!' she lashed out at him with her tongue and her hands, catching him a stinging blow to his lean, bronzed cheek and then pummelling furiously at his chest. 'Get out of here! Do you hear me? *Get out of here!*' Her voice rose along with her fury.

Court gritted his teeth, and clamping hold of her wrists pinned them behind her back with one hand, the other holding her head immobile as he dragged her so tightly against his muscular form that she felt fused to him. 'What the hell? I think I prefer you sleek and wet, anyway,' he growled as he fastened his mouth over hers.

Unable to escape the possessive contact, Eden felt her worst fears abruptly realised when, in spite of all her resentment and fury and her determination to refuse him the satisfaction of a response, she still couldn't deny the rising tide of sensation he was relentlessly evoking within her. Or the fact that she *wanted* to kiss him back.

It was a combination she could fight against for only so long, and then with a helpless sob of part surrender, part arousal her lips parted beneath the vibrant pressure of his and she strained to free her hands in order to link them about him. Reacting to her response, Court loosened his hold and her fingers promptly sought the muscularly firm, smooth skin beneath his shirt, delighting in the feel of him, and experiencing a sudden unexpected but exhilarating sense of power when his arms hardened about her convulsively at her touch.

His mouth traced a burning path down her arching throat to her shoulder and lower, his hands slowly caressing her damp skin, cupping her breasts and softly tormenting her nipples so that she clung to him weakly, a feeling of abandon, of sensuous longing overwhelming her. Gathering her up into his arms, Court moved across to the nearest bed, settling his long length beside her curving form and reclaiming her lips with a consuming passion even as his hands began divesting them both of their restraining clothing.

For Eden there was no holding back, and any thought of refusing him was long forgotten as she gave herself up to the new and exciting sensations he was awakening within her. The feel of his bare skin next to hers sent a warm rush of desire coursing through her, and she knew the satisfaction of giving him pleasure too when he groaned as she trailed her hands over the darkly tanned flesh of his back and chest. Never in her life had she been so close to any man before, and she savoured every new experience with a rapturous sense of wonder.

'Oh, God, you don't know what you do to me!' Court murmured hoarsely as he raised his head to gaze down at her, his aquamarine eyes heavy with a smouldering desire as they scanned her honey-tinted, naked form.

Self-consciously, instinctively, Eden made to shield herself, but he caught her hands gently to stop her. 'No. Let me look at you,' he entreated softly. 'You're just so damned beautiful!'

Although she flushed slightly, Eden made no further move to cover herself, but her lashes did fan down shyly on to her cheeks. 'I think—you are too.' She hesitated, never having said anything of the kind to a man previously. 'And I—like you touching me,' she owned on a tremulous breath, and promptly reddened further.

'No more than I do, believe me!' he declared thickly, and as if to prove the point, smoothed his hand down over her flat stomach to her hip and the curve of her thigh.

Eden quivered, a warm ache radiating out from the pit of her stomach. She wanted to touch him too in much the same way, but when her exploring fingers reached the muscled hardness of his stomach she found the experience just too new, too unfamiliar for her to proceed further—and it showed in the changing expressions that crossed her face.

Watching them, Court suddenly stiffened, and then caught her to him tightly. 'Oh, God!' he groaned against her temple. 'He lied, didn't he?'

'Wh-who?' she tilted her head upwards to query in bewilderment.

'Alick!' The word snapped from his throat like the crack of a whip.

'About what?'

She could feel his chest rise and fall sharply. 'You and him having been lovers!'

Eden sucked in a shocked breath. 'He actually said we had been?'

'Maybe not in so many words, but he certainly damned well did by implication in refusing to deny it when asked, and continually referring to you as someone very special to him!'

It explained so much, but. . . she had trusted him to at least make some attempt to clarify their true relationship! 'I'll kill him!' she vowed wrathfully, and for the second time that day.

'You'll have to wait your turn!' Court gritted. 'God, I've felt like decking him on a couple of occasions when he's dumped his more troublesome birds out here in the past, but this time I might just go ahead and do it!' His eyes glinted with an ominous light.

Eden bit at her lip, worried about being the cause of trouble between the two of them, even though it hadn't been of her actual making. 'But why would he do such a thing?'

'Who knows?' He made a disparaging sound. 'Perhaps his reputation just made it impossible for him to admit that he hadn't been able to make the grade with the most beautiful of all the girls he's—honoured us with!' As he gazed down at her, both his expression and his voice gentled. 'Because you're definitely that, believe me!'

Warmed that he should think so, she felt more able to at least say something on Alick's behalf. 'Although from something he said this afternoon, I think he did mean to tell you the truth. . . if a little belatedly.'

'Oh?' His brows peaked expressively. 'Then why didn't he? He certainly had the opportunity to before dinner.'

Remembering why had her dropping her gaze uncomfortably, but in all fairness still feeling obliged to disclose, 'Because I—said I didn't want him to.' She continued hurriedly, 'Not that I realised at the time all that apparently needed to be explained.'

'*You* stopped him?' Court frowned at her uncomprehendingly. 'For crying out loud, why?'

Not confident enough even now to completely divulge her feelings, Eden hedged, 'Because I only discovered this morning that you believed I'd had an affair with him, and my pride just rebelled at the thought of being put in the position of defending myself, when it just wasn't true in the first place.' In the hope of forestalling any further question he might voice, she rushed to ask one of her own. 'So what made you finally realise I wasn't one of Alick's ex-girl-friends, anyhow?'

Court smiled lazily, and had her heart turning over in her chest. 'Just the fact that you suddenly showed an inexperience and an embarrassment that no one who was used to such intimate situations would have done.' He stroked a finger along the line of her jaw, his expression sobering. 'I just wish I'd realised it sooner.'

She swallowed, and queried with bated breath, 'Why?'

He shifted so that he was leaning over her, and his lips lowered to hers in a long, searing kiss that left them both breathing heavily. 'Because I love you!' he confessed huskily. 'Because you're the one female I can't get out of my mind and I can't live without. Because I've been as jealous as hell at the thought of Alick having known you first, and because I've gone through purgatory trying to fight it. And last, although by no means least, because I want you as my wife!' He shook his head ruefully and smoothed back her tousled hair with a gentle hand. 'That was why I came after you tonight. To do anything I had to—ask, persuade, force—in order to get you to marry me. It suddenly didn't matter any more whether you and Alick had been lovers or not. I just knew I wanted you—as you were—and to hell with whatever had gone before!' He inclined his head slightly, but the gaze that held hers she had never thought to see so unsure. 'So, will you marry me, Golden Girl?'

Eden wrapped her arms about his neck, her eyes shining mistily. 'Oh, Court. . . yes!' she sighed, that once aggravating nickname all of a sudden taking on an entirely different implication. 'I think I've loved you since that first day you kissed me, only I didn't believe there was a chance of you ever feeling the same about me.' She eyed him reproachfully. 'Especially not after you made dinner this evening the most miserable experience of my entire life!'

His mouth shaped wryly, apologetically. 'I'm sorry, love, but if it's any consolation, I didn't derive any pleasure from it either, because I was finding that the worse I knew I made you feel, the worse I felt myself. Which is somewhat self-defeating!' drily. 'I'm afraid that after seeing you in tears when you left Alick, and believing it to be for the reason I did, then I just wasn't in any frame of mind to either control my thoughts or my rampant feelings. That is, not until you started to leave the homestead, when I suddenly realised that all I was succeeding in doing was to drive you further away, when all I really wanted was to have you with me. . . for always!' He pressed a kiss against the corner of her mouth. 'Forgive me?'

'For wanting to have me with you?' she ventured to tease.

'Never that!' he claimed deeply, and this time set his lips to the sweetly scented hollow at the base of her throat. When he raised his head again, it was to gaze at her quizzically. 'But as it evidently wasn't because of Alick, why were you crying this afternoon?'

'Because it didn't look as if the gorgeous male I was in love with would ever want to have anything to do with me!' she relayed with mock vexation.

'Oh, there's lots I'd like to do with you,' Court growled, the look in his darkening eyes most explicit.

Her answering smile was piquant. 'But won't your family be wondering where you are?'

'I suspect they've already got a fair idea,' he drawled on a dry note. 'And it's just as it's going to be in future too.' His voice deepened as he began lowering his head to hers. '*I'll* be wherever you are.'

Eden sighed blissfully. It was a prospect she could find no fault with whatsoever.

It was a misunderstanding that could cost a young woman her
virtue, and a notorious rake his heart.

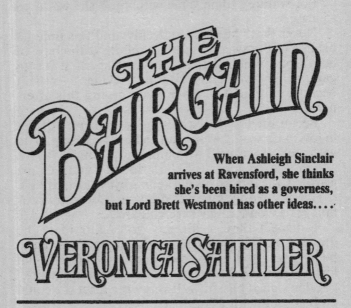

THE BARGAIN

When Ashleigh Sinclair
arrives at Ravensford, she thinks
she's been hired as a governess,
but Lord Brett Westmont has other ideas....

VERONICA SATTLER

ATTRACTIVE, SPACE SAVING BOOK RACK

Display your most prized novels on this handsome and sturdy book rack. The hand-rubbed walnut finish will blend into your library decor with quiet elegance, providing a practical organizer for your favorite hard-or soft-covered books.

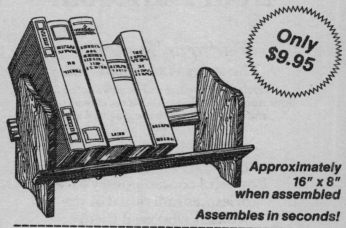

Only $9.95

Approximately 16" x 8" when assembled

Assembles in seconds!

To order, rush your name, address and zip code, along with a check or money order for $10.70* ($9.95 plus 75¢ postage and handling) payable to *Harlequin Reader Service*:

Harlequin Reader Service
Book Rack Offer
901 Fuhrmann Blvd.
P.O. Box 1396
Buffalo, NY 14269-1396

Offer not available in Canada.

BKR-1A

*New York and Iowa residents add appropriate sales tax.

Six exciting series for you every month... from Harlequin

Harlequin Romance·
The series that started it all

Tender, captivating and heartwarming...
love stories that sweep you off to faraway places
and delight you with the magic of love.

◆

Harlequin Presents·
Powerful contemporary love stories...as individual as the women who read them

The No. 1 romance series...
exciting love stories for you, the woman of today...
a rare blend of passion and dramatic realism.

◆

Harlequin Superromance®
It's more than romance... it's Harlequin Superromance

A sophisticated, contemporary romance-fiction
series, providing you with a longer,
more involving read...a richer mix of complex plots,
realism and adventure.

Harlequin Romance

Coming Next Month

2875 THE WAITING HEART Jeanne Allan
City schoolteacher Susan's Christmas holiday at the Colorado ranch of her elderly friend Elizabeth is spoiled by Elizabeth's son—a man who dominates everything and everyone. Expecting to dominate Susan, too, he's surprised by her equally strong resistance!

2876 THE HEART OF THE MATTER Lindsay Armstrong
All her young life Clarry has turned to Robert for help, so it seems entirely natural when he saves her family home by marrying her. Only now there is a price to pay—Clarry has to grow up....

2877 HEARTLAND Bethany Campbell
Budding cartoonist Toby is glad to help temporarily injured top cartoonist Jake Ulrick—but it isn't easy. Cold, abrupt, a tyrant to work for, he resents needing anyone. So it doesn't help matters at all when Toby falls in love with him.

2878 AN ENGAGEMENT IS ANNOUNCED Claudia Jameson
Physiotherapist Anthea Norman cuts short her Canary Islands visit when her hostess's attractive lawyer nephew zooms in for serious pursuit. Instinct tells her to run. She doesn't want to experience the heartbreak of loving and losing again....

2879 SELL ME A DREAM Leigh Michaels
Stephanie has built a career for herself in real estate as well as made a home for her small daughter—the daughter Jordan doesn't know about. And she's practically engaged to staid dependable Tony. Now isn't the time for Jordan to come bouncing back into her life.

2880 NO SAD SONG Alison York
To achieve success in her operatic career, Annabel has to work with Piers Bellingham, the top entrepreneur—and a man she detests. As it turns out, working with Piers is not the problem. It's strictly one of the heart!

Available in December wherever paperback books are sold, or through Harlequin Reader Service.

In the U.S.
901 Fuhrmann Blvd.
P.O. Box 1397
Buffalo, N.Y. 14240-1397

In Canada
P.O. Box 603
Fort Erie, Ontario
L2A 5X3